THE
SHARECROPPER'S
—SON—

OTHER BOOKS BY JOHN V. AMODEO

Voices of Hell's Kitchen

Believe—Journey from Jacksonville

Blessed or Cursed

The Captain's Coin

Revolutionary War Series: Francis Lewis

THE
SHARECROPPER'S
SON

JOHN V. AMODEO

Copyright © 2016 John V. Amodeo.

All rights reserved. No part of this book may be used or reproduced by any means, graphic, electronic, or mechanical, including photocopying, recording, taping or by any information storage retrieval system without the written permission of the author except in the case of brief quotations embodied in critical articles and reviews.

Archway Publishing books may be ordered through booksellers or by contacting:

Archway Publishing
1663 Liberty Drive
Bloomington, IN 47403
www.archwaypublishing.com
1 (888) 242-5904

Because of the dynamic nature of the Internet, any web addresses or links contained in this book may have changed since publication and may no longer be valid. The views expressed in this work are solely those of the author and do not necessarily reflect the views of the publisher, and the publisher hereby disclaims any responsibility for them.

Any people depicted in stock imagery provided by Thinkstock are models, and such images are being used for illustrative purposes only.
Certain stock imagery © Thinkstock.

ISBN: 978-1-4808-3342-5 (sc)
ISBN: 978-1-4808-3343-2 (e)

Library of Congress Control Number: 2016910414

Print information available on the last page.

Archway Publishing rev. date: 7/13/2016

To the people of the Mississippi delta

ACKNOWLEDGMENTS

Writing a historical novel about the Jim Crow South was a challenge that I enjoyed. Getting information on actual events and applying them to a fictional character was an enjoyable and learning experience. Such an endeavor would not have been possible without the encouragement, suggestion, and support from family, friends, and professional colleagues.

Michele Lee, librarian at Manhattan's Mercy College, was especially helpful. I would be remiss if I didn't thank her for her time, expertise, and advice. I am grateful to call her a colleague and friend.

Lawrence Blake Group International, led by L. Blake Harvey, was there from the start. Acting as a publicist, Blake provided important suggestions and helped formulate the text. I am grateful to the professionalism of his staff and the support they provided when it came to revisions and copyright issues.

In addition, I want to thank the New-York Historical Society for their help and encouragement. I was able to delve into the archives and obtain pertinent information. This helped to add to the dynamic and make the text more relevant and interesting.

The New York Public Library's main Forty-Second Street location is a great repository for any historian, and I'm grateful to the competent staff that was so helpful. Working in the main room is an experience in itself. Being surrounded by such beautiful mosaics was indeed motivational.

I also wish to thank the many friends who were so supportive: Fr. Own Lafferty, Lee Collings, Jerry Adam, Gerard Guglielmo, Dr. Marge Valleau, Ed Bruhn, Paula Stark, Mary Ann Gibson, Carol Hollenbeck, Amos Moore Jr., Dr. Patrick Burke, the Scripture Group at Holy Cross Church headed by Ed Green, and the students at Mercy College.

Finally, I wish to thank my family, especially my sisters, Carol Krajewski and Linda Gulli, cousin Margaret Hipwell, and nephew, Ed Krajewski.

To you all, a most hearty thank you!

John V. Amodeo

CONTENTS

Chapter 1—Life in the Mississippi Delta 1
Chapter 2—October 7 5
Chapter 3—Sharecropping on Crawley's Land 15
Chapter 4—Hurley's General Store 23
Chapter 5—Draft Notice 31
Chapter 6—Home 37
Chapter 7—Draft Board Inductee 45
Chapter 8—Trip to Basic Training 52
Chapter 9—Basic Training 62
Chapter 10—Leader of the Pack 69
Chapter 11—Singing Troupe at Basic 79
Chapter 12—Orders "Over There" 89
Chapter 13—Leviathan 95
Chapter 14—Crossing the Atlantic 101
Chapter 15—Performing on Board 108
Chapter 16—France 117
Chapter 17—Trench Warfare 124
Chapter 18—Armistice 133
Chapter 19—Paris 141

Chapter 20—Le Chat Noir 148
Chapter 21—Fame in Paris 155
Chapter 22—Marie 163
Chapter 23—Marriage 170
Chapter 24—Back in the Delta..176
Chapter 25—Paris Bound 181
Chapter 26—Legacy.. 187

CHAPTER 1

Life in the Mississippi delta never seemed to change. For most people, the world was the delta. The delta was dominated by the "Father of all rivers"—the Mississippi. People were born there, raised there, and died there. Nothing else was expected from them. The land was lord and master and controlled their lives. It was an existence that fate had designed. From generation to generation, for the people of the delta, it was as if time itself had stood still.

The delta! The region that stretches from Memphis upriver down to Vicksburg, long and flat with rich cotton fields that had witnessed events, good and bad, that resonate to this day. The land controlled the destiny of all. Determined and always in charge, it dictated your life. Like it or not, residents of the delta were beholden to the land. And the land dictated all.

Never straying far from home, the poor blacks and whites in post–Civil War America had a wretched existence. Sharecropping had replaced slavery for the blacks. In the old days, in the post–Reconstruction Era after 1877, each day was a continuation of the day before. The only changes were the seasons and the generations that came and went. Routine after routine of getting up at the break of dawn and working till the sun went down.

There was no escaping the delta's tight grasp. Powerful and uncompromising, it would make or break you. It made decisions, important decisions that kept families together or drove them apart. Its powerful hands gripped the worker, making his wretched existence dependent on him.

Hard work. Back-breaking work. Tilling the red soil on a small patch of land just to eke out a meager existence. Generation after generation depended on the land. Nothing seemed to change. The land seemed to be in charge, and the elements of sun, wind, and rain dictated one's life. The land's grip never gave in. Indeed, as lord and master, the people working it land were forever dependent on it. Whether landlord or tiller, rich or poor, black or white, one was dependent on the land. Seasons came and went, yet the drudgery of hard work was the constant determiner of one's fate. Whether you ate or not was not for you to decide. That power was given to nature. One had no choice but to bow down to the forces of nature. Yes, the land was lord and master. Your existence totally depended on it.

Work! The same monotonous work day in and day out. Life seemed never to change. Day after day—same as before. Each day like the rest. The soil tilled with the same old tools handed down from generation to generation; the tools shared a macabre linkage to the past. These old, worn tools—old tools that long needed to be replaced. Tools that had rusted badly in the searing sun after being left out too long in the steady, soaking rain. Rusty and worn, the tools, like the people tilling the land, had seen it all. They had witnessed so much. If only these tools could tell us who tilled the soil with them year after year, decade after decade. They could relate to us so much. The drudgery under the constant eye of the overseer and the threat of losing it all. So much indeed could be told.

Day after day, year after year, the crops were planted and were eventually plucked from the wet, red clay soil and stacked and put on wagons to go to markets near and far. Cotton was still the king as it was in days past. Nothing indeed changed. Just different hands tilled the soil over the years.

King cotton; the crop sent to market to be woven into fabrics in factories far away. No mention of thanks was ever given to the nimble, often deeply calloused hands that plucked the precious cargo from the earth. The unforgiving, scorching summer sun challenged young and old. The wet, cold fall days outside whose cargo, fully loaded, was the result of long, monotonous hours of work.

The great stores in the urban north and west displayed the colorful fabrics for the prosperous consumer. No credit was given to the industrious field hands down in the delta who made it all possible. Expendable and exploited, their stories known only to their families, they remained largely unknown. They were the salt of the earth yet forgotten by history. Never given much credit, they remained an elusive part of the story that is America.

Hard work. Yes, indeed! Sharecropping became the way of life. Most of the work was done with labor gangs assigned to do the most menial to the most difficult tasks. And like most sharecroppers, Jeremiah Hayes and his family wanted their own land. Yet the landlord kept them in bondage. He owned the land they lived on, the land they worked on, owned the supplies they used and owned the supply store where they bought their products and food.

The small plot allotted to the Hayes family was indicative of the system that kept people at subsistence level. When his son James was seven years old, Jeremiah said to him, "They give a bit of land and allow us to grow a few crops, son. Yet, we're beholden to the man, plain and simple."

Sharecropping was back-breaking work. Day after day, the same routine. Nothing changed. World events came and went, and little was understood by the workers trying to live on subsistence farming. But it did finally change for one person in the delta.

The Hayes family was one of many who were a product of the delta and beholden to its grip—a family consisting of Jeremiah and Lula Mae Hayes and their two sons, James Moore Hayes and Nathaniel Jesse Hayes. Like most of the families in the delta, they were poor sharecroppers. And like most of the other sharecroppers in the area, they worked the land and received a patch of land to live and grow crops on. A typical, poor, black family in the delta. Good people, they expected nothing and remained a close family. They were united in their faith and in the hope of a better life that never seemed to come about. But events were about to change. At least for one member of the family.

It happened one October morning; October 7, to be precise, in the year 1917. That date would change the world for one young, unknown delta resident—James Hayes, the eldest son of Jeremiah and Lula Mae Hayes.

CHAPTER 2

October 7 started off like any other day. It was a Tuesday, and that meant just another day of hard work in the fields. Events would soon take over for James—events that would change his life forever. That date that would remain in the eighteen-year-old's head for the rest of his life.

It started off with no warning that this was the day that would change his life. The unexpected often creeps into our lives and shapes our destiny. When we least expect it, events can overwhelm us, resulting in transforming one's life. Surprises come whether welcomed or not. It was a complete surprise, with no warning. And this was destined to be one of those dates that demanded and got attention. Like it or not, James Hayes's life was indeed about to change. He had no control over it. It was a date that would change the life of the young Mississippi sharecropper James Hayes, who up to this moment was just another delta resident whose life was dictated by circumstances of birth and race. And then came October 7.

His fate, like many before him, had already been decided by his place of birth. Sharecropping, imposed on ex-slaves and poor whites, remained a form of subsistence agriculture well into the twentieth century. A meager and back-breaking job, it kept many in the delta beholden to the large landowners. Such was the case for young James on that fateful date.

The day started with the usual routines. It was all so strange. The date—October 7—was just another day. Nothing special. Or was it?

James Hayes was up and out of bed at six. It was still dark outside. The hoot owl's faint refrain was a soothing sound. Almost a ritual, James waited to hear the owl's hoots grow fainter as the sun came up. He knew then it was his time to rise. With no electricity or running water, his day began as it had for many of his ancestors in the delta for years—getting up and facing the outdoor elements.

The place he called home was anything but comfortable in its furnishings. The bed he shared with his sixteen-year-old brother, Nathaniel, had seen better days. The lumpy, well-worn mattress always challenged him to get a good night's sleep. Added to the mix were his brother's constant, deep snores that sometimes awakened him before he could hear the owl in the oft-distant dogwood trees start its song. Getting out of bed was a rude ritual—his bare feet hitting the cool floor as he headed out the door, putting on his well-worn blue overhauls.

Dawn! Another day to work on the Crawley land, the land that his father, grandfather, and previous generations of the Hayes family had done generation after generation, beginning from slave days and beyond. Then, with the advent of Reconstruction after the Civil War ended in 1865, the substitute existence of sharecropping came upon the scene, which was not much better. Sharecropping was a very meager existence based on giving and taking. For James and the other young black men who were reared in the delta, life had indeed already been decided for them—life that would be hard, cruel, and often unfair.

Deep inside, James desperately wanted out and longed to break free. He thought of the ones who had managed to go north in search of a job and better life. Yet, it was not to be for the young man. Like most young men, he wanted to leave this miserable delta for a better place. And like most young men, he had dreams! Yet he had issues dealing with his family.

He was the eldest son. He felt he owed his parents at least a hand until he was able to break free, perhaps marry and leave Mississippi and head north to Chicago, as did his Uncle Moses two years earlier. His uncle wrote and told of jobs and housing and opportunities. It was a dream and a goal for James. The big city with its lights, music joints, pool hall clubs, cinema attractions, different people of all backgrounds, and of course, the women! The hustle. The constant challenges that awaited one who ventured out of this existence. He dreamed of the big city, and it kept him going during the darkest moments.

It sounded so good. He heard stories of the money could be made, cars bought, and maybe even owning a house. But right now, however, that had to put on hold. He had to assist his family—his father, Jeremiah, who had worked too long in the sun and was now very tired. His wrinkled face made hard by the hot sun gave the appearance of a man older than his forty-three years. Deliberate in his step as a result of a tractor accident that crushed his left large toe three years earlier, he was often in constant pain. His dependence on his sons was evident. A certain amount of guilt always stopped James from abruptly leaving and heading on the next train north.

James had a dilemma, knowing he wanted out of this meager existence, but he felt loyalty to his kin. It kept him up at nights thinking about his future. The sights and smells of the big city and the colored lights would remain a dream for now. Yet, James's imagination would take over and he envisioned himself, dressed in a Sunday suit, walking proudly down the street. He could feel a sense of awe and power as people spoke to him, and he, tipping his broad hat, would smile back. It was a momentary escape for the young James, who knew the pull of the unknown was a dream that indeed had to wait for now. But he looked forward to the eventual ride on the train up north and what lay beyond. Freedom! A first big step out into the world. He was ready for that ride—so ready and eager to take it! But it had to be put on hold. He had his family and, ever the loyal son, would remain in the delta for the foreseeable future.

His younger asthmatic brother couldn't keep up with him in the cotton field on the Crawley land. Nathaniel's restless nights and difficulty getting his breath were acerbated year after year of constantly inhaling of cotton lint in the fields. Sorting out the cotton and placing it into stacks, he often had to stop and catch his breath. He was a sick young man and yet, he couldn't get his condition attended to. His family needed him to do his part. The doctors would have to wait. He tried so hard. He didn't want to disappoint his older brother and father. But his condition wouldn't allow him to keep up. So, it was up to James to make sure the family had food on the table and was able to get by. Since his dad's accident, the family was more dependent on him.

Nathaniel did have some assets. He shared a keen eye, and like his older brother, he could shoot the well-worn rifle the family had. Often the brothers would surprise their mother with a squirrel, rabbit, or possum to cook. Taking the old Colt rifle, they would take turns at shooting down pheasants or wild game, such as the occasional turkey, dove, quail, or errant chicken. Their mother tilled the small patch of land where they had a small coop with three hens. Lula Mae grew turnips, soybeans, and string beans, which came in handy when events were not good. But it was the boys who prided themselves as sharpshooters. They loved to show off. When they brought home a surprise turkey or dove, they were greeted by their grateful mother. They helped pluck and gut it and knew they were in for fresh meat—a real treat. It saved their mother from scrimping to put together a meal befitting her hungry lot.

On occasion, usually on Sundays, they both would fish in the fast-moving local creek, which had good runoff from the adjoining hill on its way to drain into the mighty Mississippi, just a quarter mile west. Using a simple, homemade rod, they attached a worm as bait and were adept at getting catfish, sun fish, and assorted varieties of small fish that would give the family added fresh food.

Like most sharecroppers, the Hayes family was beholden to the owner, the ex-slave family Crawley, whose roots, like the Hayes' went back many generations. The current Crawley proprietor was Warren Crawley, a fifty-one-year-old hard line, no-nonsense man. Much like his father and other white proprietors in the delta, he was demanding and uncompromising. He didn't like surprises and expected much from his employees. At six foot two, he made a commanding presence with a booming voice often laced with profanities. He was feared by most of his help lest they be replaced. James Hayes could see right through him and knew he was a controlling, cold person. "Every time I look at him,

I see our wretched past." James vowed he would one day confront him. For now, it was not to be. Reality set in, and it was time to face the day.

James got up and went to the basin after using the outhouse, washing his face and hands and put on a faded red flannel shirt that had seen better days.

Grabbing the towel, he looked in the faded mirror at his unshaven face and smiled. He had confidence and self-pride and knew he had to do something with his life. He liked what he saw in the foggy mirror above the tin basin. Despite his present circumstance, he had confidence in himself, a trait handed down from his maternal side. Yes, he wanted out but not now. His mother, always mindful of the circumstances of their life, would relate the tragic story of his Uncle Franklin.

Uncle Franklin Joyner defended a young man wrongly accused of stealing. The details were always sketchy; many in the black community felt he was set up. He was known as an agitator and someone not afraid to confront injustice. Franklin, known as an outspoken troublemaker to the established order, questioned authority and had challenged his landlord over salaries to the hired hands, many of whom didn't read. In the era long before Miranda rights, little was needed to bring charges against anyone suspected of the slightest infraction—especially if you were black and in Mississippi.

He demanded that the sheriff investigate and arrest the right person. Joyner was a witness to the actual theft. Yet, he was no snitch. He didn't want an innocent someone going off to the chain gang. Yes, he knew who the real thief was, but it was not to be. The wrong person, a friend of Franklin's named Willie Jones, was arrested instead of the actual thief, Henry Clayton. Like Joyner, Jones too was known as someone who was a troublemaker. Joyner called the inaction by the sheriff, once Jones was in custody, a "complete sham."

"He ain't worth calling himself a sheriff," he boasted aloud, not knowing that a few of the white patrons overheard him.

Jones was never liked at the local stores and in the field. Always demanding the correct change and like, Joyner, not afraid to speak up when a poor, illiterate customer got shortchanged at stores, he was always someone that the "good ol' boys" network took notice of.

Joyner's bold statement made its way back to the sheriff, Clayton King, and once he found out, he was a marked man. Franklin Joyner knew he had to do something. He was told to pack up and leave Hinds County but never made it out. Meanwhile, Willie Jones's fate was already sealed. He would soon be dispatched to a road chain gang. Joyner was another situation. He had to get out and get out fast.

By resorting to such bold action, Joyner too was a marked man and disappeared for two days until his limp body was found in the wooded area just a few miles from where he lived, hanging from a cottonwood tree. James's mother was just a young girl in 1899 when the lynching took place but never forgot the impact it had on the family. Lula Mae always brought up this sordid and brutal event whenever her eldest James got "too jumpy." She always told of the pain and anger and scare that the lynching of her uncle brought.

"My poor grandma never got over her son killed like that and died within eight months."

James was careful but knew he couldn't deal much longer with the Jim Crow world of Mississippi of 1917. He was determined he would never end up like his Uncle Franklin.

Stepping outside the cabin for the second time, he noticed the dew was unusually moist and cool as his bare feet touched the soil. The dew looked like cob webs, forming a grayish hue over the fields as far as the eye could see. He knew what this meant. Autumn would soon give way to winter and the cold. But the grass felt good beneath his bare feet as he headed back into the shack. The leaves were already giving up their green hue and turning the land into a variegated landscape of different colors. But today's business in the fields had to be attended to, and he momentarily forgot about the pending onslaught of the wet, rainy, and cool winter about to come to the delta.

He lived in the wooden, one-story cabin his grandfather had built it on the Crawley property not far from the banks of the Yazoo River in 1871. It was a shack without the benefits of electricity and running water. The fireplace was the focal point for his mom, and she spent most of her time preparing meals there for her husband and sons. With the outhouse and a well for running water nearby, the cabin remained a simple albeit humble domicile for the struggling family. It was home, and the family made the best with their meager furnishings. The cabin, with its two small bedrooms, was in need of repairs. It had been seen better days.

With the advent of sharecropping and with the help of "Yankee money" during Reconstruction, the Hayes family had a patch of land ceded to them from the Crawley plantation to grow a few crops while still working the Crawley land half mile up the ridge. His mother had shared the simple, unpainted hovel with her husband of twenty-one years, Jeremiah Hayes, and son Nathaniel. Like her husband, Lula Mae was a product of the delta, having met Jeremiah working the fields in a nearby farmstead.

It was 6:15. The sun started to shine into the cracks of the place the Hayes family called home. Today indeed promised another day of hard labor. The sun wouldn't be so intense this time of year, so the work wouldn't feel quite as demanding. But work was work. James's mother knew her sons were in need of a hearty breakfast before heading out to Mr. Warren Crawley's land to till the soil.

Mr. Warren, as he was known in these parts, was said to be a secret member of the local chapter of the KKK. No one ever said a word neither in the field or in the Hayes household about it. Yet the rumors were always there.

He once remarked to James's dad, "I can get any darkie to work for me. Tell your sons they have to be here on time!"

Threats of idleness shook Jeremiah up. He remembered his grandfather's stories of the old days, the brutality of the slave days, and the problems imposed once the Yankees left in 1872. Jeremiah too demanded his sons be up and ready to do their part. Despite Nathaniel's delicate health, both had to head to the nearby field. They had no other option.

As he walked on the wooden floor, each step he made creaked

loudly. The years hadn't been kind to the old shack. With every hard rain, a few buckets had to be placed in at least two spots by the curtainless window adjacent to the only door. James wanted to make repairs and give the entire outside a coat of paint, but his father countered by telling him that would be a luxury for a future date.

"Don't have the coins, boy, for this. I need to keep the family intact and have food on the table. Once you make a few bucks, then we'll talk about getting the place a paint job and other things for your mom."

Like most residents of the delta, Jeremiah had come to realize that his sons had to accept what fate had dictated. A realist, he never wavered in his love for them. Yet he was aware of the special challenges that this life had to endure. He wanted better for his family and yet was tied to his land as was his forbearers.

James Hayes was another story! His son took after his mother side of the family—the Moores. It was a family that had a quite a history of rebellion with often disastrous results. The lynching of her uncle always in the back of her mind, Lula Mae, protective yet assertive, would add: "We don't talk about your uncle outside this house, you hear?" The message was clear. Keep issues close to you, and don't let anyone hear you mouth off. James knew otherwise. He would smile, giving his mom her piece to say, and move on.

At eighteen, James Moore Hayes had grown to six foot one, 190 pounds of taut muscle from years tilling the fields and picking up bales of cotton and soybean and other assorted crops grown on the former Crawley plantation. Other workers marveled at his prowess. The young girls would watch him in the summer sun without his shirt on. His infectious smile complemented a thick mat of hair and handsome face with high cheekbones and dark, seductive eyes. His skin tone in the sun was velvety bronze. The young ladies would stare and smile, and James, liking the attention, would wink back as the girls, giggling, would pick up their pace and move on. He liked the attention and knew he could get his pick from the available females tilling the soil near and about him. He could be a ladies man and often daydreamed of having a few ladies at his disposal.

But that dream would have to wait. Now, he had to attend to his family and provide for them.

Because of his strength and bravado, James was always in demand whenever the bales were tied and the crew needed to place the cotton on the wagons headed for nearby Yazoo City.

Now, having finished grooming up a bit, he headed to the sole, rectangular table in the center of the cabin. The smell of his mom's corn bread and coffee hastened his pace. A broad smile followed by the daily ritual of giving his mom a kiss on the cheek and a big "good morning,' to his seated brother and father.

"You're always late, bro," Nathaniel dryly remarked to James, a smile on his face.

James was ready to start his day. This time of day, the family always sat down, said grace, and had a good sendoff thanks to his mom's attention to detail in preparing a good breakfast. His young brother's attempt at humor didn't go over all well. Clearly irritated, James pushed the rickety chair forcibly from under the creaky wooden table to sit, giving his younger brother a look that his attempt at humor was not appreciated. Yet, it was all theatrics. James loved being the center of attention whatever circumstances prevailed.

"I don't need to hear this from you, little one!" He looked at his mother and gave her a wide smile. She knew the deal—two brothers bantering before heading to the tasks at hand. It was an ease of tension before a long day of toil.

"Eat up. I know this is a busy time of year before the weather changes." Jeremiah, picking up his large mug of coffee, nodded at his wife and said to his boys, "You been working hard out there. I don't like it. I wish you could be in that school."

"Nah, don't need any more schooling. I can read and write, and I don't need much more," James said, looking at his mom with a clear frown on her face.

Shaking her head she said, "I know I didn't raise any preachers in this family! You're bound to work the fields until something comes your way …"

"Mom, don't worry. I gots enough education. I know that Pop's injury makes it hard for you." James wanted to reassure his parents. "Besides, I want to try to save up."

"For what?" his younger brother asked.

"Don't know, little bro, but I know I'm going to need some cash for the future." His mother, wiping her hands on her apron, approached the table. Jeremiah chimed in to reassure his sons that he knew what the deal was.

"I know that. But you be picking up the slack. My accident has left me limping and in constant pain, but we gots to pay the man and get the bills paid and …"

James's mother again wiped her apron and placed more hot corn muffins on the on the table, interrupting her husband and adding, "I don't want any of this talk at this table, y'all hear?" Her eyes followed each of the men at the table, who exchanged glances and knew it was time to eat up and nothing more. Mom had spoken!

"Yes, ma'am." Nathaniel had already applied a good serving of butter to the hot muffin.

Lula Mae had returned to the warm fireplace with a hearty supply of fresh eggs hatched the night before. Looking at Nathaniel, his smile momentarily catching his mother off-guard, she returned the smile and sat down to join her family. It would soon be time to get to the Crawley land.

CHAPTER 3

James and Nathaniel set off to work. Since their father's accident, Jeremiah used an improvised walking stick that James had assembled from a branch of an elm tree to steady his gait. It did its job as it made it easier for the proud father to move around despite the chronic pain from an unhealed injury. James looked back on occasion as they took the familiar path that led to the fields that so many before had toiled. He knew his dad's unattended leg had left a permanent limp coupled with pain with his every step. Torn and at times angry at his life, James, like his father, felt attached to the land, knowing that it was the only means to help his family. Yet, James wanted out so badly! Little did he know that this day—October 7—would be a new beginning for him.

The walk to the Crawley fields would take just six to ten minutes, depending on their pace and eagerness to start the day's work. These fields had witnessed so much drama in the past. It was indicative of the large tracts of agrarian Deep South that produced profits at the forced expense of slave labor in antebellum South. Crawley's large acreage of land demanded much manual labor now, as it had in the past. Picking and sorting out cotton was still done the same way, day after day, year after year.

Despite the advancement of farming and the onset of the automobile and tractor, old man Crawley still wanted his product to go to market from the twenty-two people in his employ like it had in the past.

"He's too damn cheap to buy us any new tools; do you expect him to buy a new tractor?" James's dad remarked. The old, rusty tractor that caused his father's accident was abandoned, leaving no modern convenience for the hands tilling the soil.

In reality, the advancement of such improvements vis-à-vis modern machinery speeded up the production at the expense of the labor pool. With the dismal forecast of no work, many, like Uncle Moses, had left in search of a better life in the north. Technological advances contributed to the Great Migration of blacks and poor whites from the rural South in search of a better life in the North. Workers were needed in the Ford Motor Company in Dearborn and the steel mills around Pittsburgh and the Goodyear Tire Factory in Akron and the garment industry in New York City. Jobs were the goal of these migrants and a better life devoid of the racism and paternalism dotting the southern landscape.

Most of the laborers, like the Hayes family, were beholden to Mr. Warren, as were their ancestors. The small patch of land to sharecrop adjacent to their shack was a token gesture. It allowed the family to get by and grow the few crops on their small turf of land. Throughout the South, many ex-slaves, poor whites, and the few newly arriving immigrants faced similar circumstances. Sharecropping became a way of life, dismal and subsistence as it was.

Once given the opportunity to farm, sharecroppers felt almost a loyalty to the land and the owners. Like other families, the Hayes were tied to the Crawley farmstead. Like it or not, it was a living, and the only escape was to join the now called Great Migration north that Moses and others had done to seek jobs. Either that or stay and grow old in the delta. It was on James's mind as he watched his father maneuver with difficulty toward his daily grind. *I sure as hell am not to end up like that*, he told himself often. He wanted desperately to take his whole family north in search of a better life, but it was not feasible. Without financial resources and the added drama of a new life, his family held back and stayed on.

The brothers got to the farm, and Crawley nodded, adding, "Good morning. We got a lot to do today boys."

James knew that Crawley wanted to get his bales to market and onto the barge to take it downstream to Vicksburg. His curt salutation would be the only acknowledgement of their presence. He demanded much and expected much from his hired help.

The bales would be weighed; Crawley would pay for shipment to Vicksburg and be paid per bale. More bales meant more money in his pocket. It was a constant race to get the cotton to market before other landlords arrived with the same shipment. Crawley was known to the men on the docks and generally tolerated despite his aloofness toward the workers. James hated to accompany him to the docks, as it meant more back-breaking labor with a token stipend to cover his added burden. Oftentimes he looked around at the hectic back-and-forth with cargo being loaded and thought of the places he could go if only he could stow away on one ship. The old riverboat gambling boats had long gone out, and now the steam powered barges aligned the piers. *Not the prettiest sight on the river*, thought James. But he liked the idea of going it alone and traveling and meeting new people, finding a job with extra cash in his pocket, and settling down to a comfortable life without the segregated life he was forced to endure. These trips down to the dock made him all the more antsy.

The thought always was there, but then the guilt of leaving his family to fend for themselves took over. As rough as the trips to the bank of the Mississippi were, they provided a momentary lapse in his dismal existence. It put a smile on his face and made the situation bearable, always dreaming of that escape and to explore a new life. But these dreams would have to wait for the moment.

Today's bales seemed unusually heavy. Perhaps it was due to the heavy rain that fell two nights before. The bales, still saturated with excess water, made towing them to the carts and subsequent trip to the docks all the more difficult. Looking around at the seven attached bales, he knew the other crew members had toiled hard and into the night before. He often worked with his nearby neighbors. They were not as strong as he, yet they were a comfort and source of communication. Often breaking into gospel songs, their presence made life a little easier.

James could belt out a tune in a basso profoundo voice. His favorite was, "Swing Low, Sweet Chariot." He loved the lyrics he learned at his country church whose pastor saw something in the young man. James especially liked the verse:

I looked upon the river and what did I see?

A band of angels coming forth to carry me home.

He envisioned the angel as a young, beautiful woman clad in a silk white gown in need of him. In his daydream, he would sweep her away, and they would have no cares and live a free and abundant life. It kept him going in the worst of times while humming the songs he learned in church. And the music now in the delta was taking on a unique style of old-time religious songs plus the lyrics put to a different rhythm of deliberate distortions and timbre. He could hear it in the clubs whenever he went into Vicksburg and listened intently to the new sound. He had heard of musicians going from town to town and making the new sounds of jazz available to all audiences. *Perhaps it will happen. I'll sing or strum the guitar that I have and make it at some club.* It remained an elusive dream but kept him thinking of his future as a performer.

Music would set James off to a new height. Improvised with slapping of thighs to keep a constant rhythm, unpredictable and improvised, creative lyrics would spew forth. What resulted was a new music variation born in the delta—jazz. Harmony, tone, and a constant syncopated rhythm were its elements. James was a quick learner, and soon he would have his own variation of the new music sound. Indeed, James would attract an instant crowd whenever he broke into unique style. People would join in, adding their own lyrics or just humming along. One of the older residents, hearing him lead a job crew in song, remarked, "That boy is destined for something, if only he could get his butt out of here!" Even old man Crawley, realizing that the music united the work crew, tolerated it. A few of the white sharecroppers would also join in, giving a unique and united work force toiling the hard land. Some suggested he go to the black clubs in Vicksburg and try out his style.

Ever the optimist, he would respond, "I'll have to wait 'til I'm ready."

The improvised lyrics sustained him, especially during the hot, humid summer. Sweat pouring down his face in spite of the red bandana around his brow, the vision of the young angel put a smile on his face.

Sure, the sweat sometimes got into his eyes. He could taste the salt as the sweat moved down his face and touched his lips. Momentarily caught off guard, he would stop, put down whatever load he was hauling, and wiping his brow with an oversized cloth, continue on with the monotonous task. But the lyrics and the songs! He would hum the lyrics and get others, both men and women, to sing some of the old gospel songs that had been handed down from generation to generation. For a few moments, they were totally free, and their voices were a testament to all they and those before them had endured. Crawley tolerated this grudgingly, knowing that it kept his workers from chatting and idle gossip.

As he approached the worksite, he looked to see if his friend Charles Atwood had arrived. Next to the tall and muscled James, Charles Atwood looked miscast. A diminutive, thin, short man of twenty-three, recently married and expecting his first child with Maggie Munson, he and James always got along well. Despite his stature, Charles proved to be a loyal, hardworking coworker. Although older than James, Charles looked up to James and followed orders whenever old Crawley put James in charge. He saw in Charles a friend, a coworker, and someone with a sense of fair play who was loyal to a fault.

Charles needed to tell James some startling news. James looked up as Charles, out of breath, couldn't contain his excitement.

"James, good morning! Did you hear the news?"

From the look on Charles's face, he expected to hear that someone had run afoul of the law or a friend was arrested or worse. "No, I hope it ain't something bad to start up the day," James added as he sized up his friend.

"Well, you know the war that's on?"

James, smiling and shaking his head, asked, "Don't tell me those Germans or what have you are coming after you!"

"Cut the crap, man. Even I know that people have signed up just to get outta here. You know Wilson got the draft through. I was told that some of us are going to be drafted and report to Raymond Courthouse for a physical."

Charles was clearly irritated. With a child on the way, the last thing he wanted was to leave his wife in time of need. The tension in his voice rising, James looked at his friend, knowing that he was upset at the prospect of getting a draft notice. It was time for him to make his friend feel at ease.

"How did you find out this? Where would we get the notice?"

James was starting to think—perhaps the war in Europe that the Congress in April had authorized at President Wilson's request against Germany and the other Central Powers had finally hit the rural South. And now, even black men were subject to the draft. In the Deep South, replete with its own brand of Jim Crow laws, a person of color had to be on guard whenever out in public or interacting with whites in power. That could mean the interaction at the local grocery store that would lend credit only if an account was established at the behest of the landowner for whom you worked. Deducted from your salary would be any incidentals such as soap, cleaning products like Ajax, and the occasional Baby Ruth candy bar. Life was very hard all around, and the power structure from the local sheriff to the state level was carefully orchestrated to bar any involvement by blacks. The 1896 Supreme Court decision of *Plessy v. Ferguson* gave the green light to segregation allowing for "separate but equal" facilities. Thus, the second-class hierarchical structure was sanctioned by the federal government, resulting in a rigid two-tier system from public accommodations to schools, water fountains, and eventually interstate travel. It was a tough life rife with tension and a sense of being left out. One had to be careful to defer to any white resident. That meant moving to the side to let them pass by on the street and try to avoid eye contact. But today's news from Charles might usher in a way out for James. The draft! Perhaps this was his meal ticket out of this misery.

Woodrow Wilson had Congress pass a Selective Service Act for all able man from eighteen to forty-five to report to their local draft boars. It never occurred to James that black soldiers would be inducted.

Sure, he knew the war was on and the United States had entered, but he couldn't envision black and white soldiers fighting alongside each other. Or would they? But this news gave him a new direction. It started him thinking.

He envisioned going off to war and seeing a part of the world he never would have experienced. Charles quickly brought him down to earth by adding, "You know they're sending men to boot camp and then overseas. At least, that's what I heard them talking about at Hurley's Store. They want us colored to be part. We probably won't get to fight. Just work in the mess hall and load stuff on ships. I don't wanna go with the baby coming. Don't wanna be in no war! We need to find out if the news is true ..."

"Hold on, dog; don't get ahead of yourself." James wanted to reassure his friend, who was clearly frustrated at the prospect of leaving his pregnant wife.

James noticed Crawley staring at them. He approached them, adjusting his wide-brimmed straw cap higher as he often did when he wanted attention. Nonverbal communication to the help that meant he was agitated.

Hearing part of the conversation, he nodded, walking away for a moment before turning around and returning. He was torn. They had a job to do of loading bales of cotton. Yet, Crawley also had a nineteen-year-old son. The discussion about the pending draft notice clearly caught his attention. He knew some of the talk at Hurley's was about the war and losing some of his help to the draft. He approached. His presence changed everything. James and Charles waited for him to speak. He was, after all, the lord of the realm. It was now time for him to speak up.

"What the hell are you boys chatting about? We got work to do. You wanna get paid or not?"

Crawley walked quickly away, not expecting or wanting an answer. Moreover, he knew that if the job pool of sharecroppers would shrink due to the war, he would have to come to terms with it. Right now, he wanted his orders stacked and ready for transport to Vicksburg. But like most people, he knew sooner or later the war would affect his livelihood too. It would come home, even to this very rural, remote part of the United States. He wasn't pleased but didn't know how to address the issue of a possible labor pool shortage. It worried him, but he didn't want his help to know. *It's all about the money up North and old Wilson catering to the Allies who want us in,* he thought as he picked up his pace, walking to check on the bales ready for loading.

Both Charles and James knew it was time to start work and let the world affairs stay away from them. Yet, James was most anxious to probe into the unknown. Maybe even going overseas to France! He had seen pictures in the paper at Hurley's General Store. This wretched existence might come to an end sooner rather than later—not going to Chicago to his uncle's but rather in some far-off land. Then, who knows, maybe settling in some altogether different environment. He picked up his pace and started lifting the bales onto the cart. A smile came on his face. He envisioned his angel taking him to some far-off land. Yet that look from old Crawley meant he had to finish the job. He worked with more speed, wanting to get to Hurley's to check if mail had indeed arrived for him. He didn't have to wait very long. Before his workday would end, he and several other men working on the Crawley land would find out that fate had indeed intervened. Life was about to change for all involved.

CHAPTER 4

By 4:00 p.m., the work load was finished. Bales were placed on three carts, drawn by a team of two horses each to journey to the dock at Vicksburg. It was a journey of eight miles, which would take an hour. A typical day except for the news that surfaced earlier that mail was in at Hurley's and would affect some of the work crew.

Most of the day's talk was about that special mail delivered to Hurley's. James, curious and exited over the prospect of getting out of this meager existence, was ready to go directly to the general store that served as a makeshift post office. He had mixed emotions for sure, as the prospect of getting out of the delta was juxtaposed with the inevitable leaving for sites unknown.

James was indeed very anxious to get to Hurley's, where mail was received and distributed to those who came to the store. In such a rural and remote area, the mail came twice a week and was the occasion for meetings of families scattered over a distance of five miles. Mail dates were Tuesdays and Fridays. Postal delivery was a big deal for those eager to hear from their distant kin.

Getting correspondence from family who had joined the Great Migration, the mail became a focal point to gather information and to sit and chat a spell, exchanging what the contents meant. Since many older residents didn't have any education, Mrs. Hurley or a loyal friend would read the much-awaited news. So countless events in one's family—births, baptisms, marriages, new jobs, accidents, and death—were always given the attention they deserved. Given the segregation of the times, blacks always congregated outside near one of the pickup carts. In cold and inclement weather, they would stay isolated from the fewer white patrons by gathering on the wooden porch. The porch did provide some shelter, as it was protected with an old sloping, slate roof. Nodding to one another and an occasional hello would be extent of most of the contact. Black patrons would always know "their place" and not linger inside and congregate outside on the porch or in the front of the store.

Mrs. Jane Hurley, a widow for five years, relied on her eldest daughter, Caroline, to help run the shop, which also served the post office. Like her husband, she received a small stipend from the federal government to run the postal service for the poor residents in this part of the delta. She taught her daughter how to write postal money orders. When money came in for the poor in the area from family who had migrated north, it was usually a postal money order. Caroline treated all the customers with the same respect that her mom had taught her. The special days—Tuesdays and Fridays—were indeed important to the folks in the delta area.

Yet, things hadn't changed much at the general store over the years. The store resembled a Currier and Ives lithograph circa 1890. It was a gathering place. The general store was the place that the nearby inhabitants got their supplies ranging from hardware goods to foodstuffs. It was a place to discuss local news, swap stories, tell jokes, and scan the few newspapers available to keep up on the latest world events. Yet it was a place that was attached to the landowners, as it was on Crawley property. So the general store was so much more for the people. It was their connection to the outside world. A connection to kin far off. A place for people like James Hayes to find out what was going on not only in the delta area but the greater community. An important link to the outside world before radio and television, it was a place to be seen and find out important news.

Like the Hayes family, the Hurley family was beholden to the landlord. They paid rent to Crawley. He, in turn, supplied the store with some of his products tilled by the very people who would buy from the store. Crawley controlled the type of crops grown, supervised the production, and controlled the weighing of product to market. In addition, he had sway over places like Hurley's, which made his enterprise all the more lucrative. Mrs. Hurley was no admirer of Warren Crawley but knew she had to deal with him in order to keep the store. A vicious cycle of control with unmitigated power made the landlord feared by sharecropper and renter alike.

Mrs. Jane Hurley had matured into a late middle-aged woman who, despite her acquiescence to the landlord Crawley, kept an independent streak. She was one of the few whites that the majority black clients trusted. Whenever a telegram came in for a family member that might have had major consequences, she was there to make sure the recipient was notified of any family crisis. She would send a reliable young man off with the news, giving him a token candy bar or chewing gum. To make sure he delivered the letter, she gave each messenger a store voucher. The mail recipient would sign it or mark X if unable to read the message. Upon returning, the deliverer would usually get an additional snack from a grateful Jane Hurley.

Some whites complained that she was too friendly with the older black women who came into the store. Jane made these hard-working matriarchs feel at home, inquiring about their families. But she did have sorts that she didn't like much. Jane Hurley didn't care much for the surly, foul-smelling older white males who would stay in the store by the old pot-belly stove on cold winter days and rant on with nonsensical chatter. *Race always on their mind.* She would always shake her head and move on, knowing that it was imperative for her to stay quiet.

Family was important to her, and if these "good old boys" overstayed their welcome, she would quickly remind them of the hour and head home. *They should be more attentive to their wives instead of worrying about everyone else!* Jane wouldn't allow chewing tobacco inside the store. "Disgusting habit and makes a mess!" If anyone came into the store chewing, she was quick to remind them to spit it out—outside the store. Jane Hurley was never one to mince words.

She never wavered to remind them that they had obligations to their family or job. Their Southern pride in check, most would merely nod and say, "Yes, Miss Jane" and move onto another subject. Jane Hurley was one tough albeit fair matron who took no nonsense and had little time for idle chatter. A proud Southern woman who had been through tough times, she epitomized the changes needed in race relations. Efforts at fair play and respect made her a hit with the black majority. Crawley, sensing her importance, often looked away whenever some people complained about being "too friendly to them."

A no-nonsense approach gave her respect at some cost to her. But she prided herself in running a clean, well-organized store. Anyone familiar with the store would see rows of penny candy in clean, neatly organized glass containers on the counter. Behind the counter were canned goods nicely arranged by product—white and red kidney beans, soy, black-eyed peas, and packets of sugar, molasses, and oats. Across the wooden counter the other side had an array of cloths ranging from gingham and flannel to cotton with small display of latest magazines and the Jackson *Daily Clarion Ledger*, the state's largest newspaper.

An array of products from sugar, molasses, salt, steel oats, and candies helped provide the poor clients, many of whom worked on large tracts of land like the Crawley stead. Black and white sharecroppers had a rough life, and it took a Jane Hurley to make them feel at home.

Jane, unlike the many white people, was in a position to interact more with her black customers. Blacks, in the majority, needed her patronage. Never a word was spoken of her philanthropic side lest she lose ownership from Warren Crawley, the tough old segregationist, non-wavering landlord. But she had been known to give credit to needy families, both black and white, who respected her. Never one to turn away a needy person, she was indeed aware of her own troubled past—an abandoned father who left her mother with four hungry mouths to feed. Little could be done except work on Crawley's large land tract. Not much schooling was in store for Jane, the oldest. It was her fate to work and help the destitute family. She never forgot her past, which was evident by her personal side. Self-educated, she ran the store well despite the concerns of Warren Crawley. She learned well from her late husband to balance the books and pay the creditors on time. Doubling as the post official for this remote region of the delta, she also was a quick learner. Her daughter was a great help, and on a day like this, with all the tension over the expected draft notices, Jane depended upon her.

Jane Morgan started working at age twelve with a full eight-hour day. It was hard work for anyone, yet she stayed the course and got the attention of a young man, Craig Hurley. Tall, good-looking, with a shyness she found at once appealing, they quickly became an item. With his easy manner and good looks, the young Jane at sixteen married Craig. It proved to be a blessing to her mom, as Craig's father operated Hurley's, the general store owned by Crawley and rented by Craig's dad.

Her late husband, Craig, inherited the shop from his dad when he died a few years after they married in 1896. The economic depression of 1893 had devastated parts of the South and affected the workforce, both white and black, on the Crawley land. Craig's dad helped the folks get through rough times with credit from the store and allowed families to get by during the worst times of the economic panic, 1894 till 1896. It was that spirit of helping your neighbor that Jane admired in her in-laws. A good Baptist, she looked the other way when her neighbors talked about her. Comfortable in her own skin, she had a no-nonsense attitude that was augmented by her sense of fair play.

Her husband Craig learned a lot from his dad, who molded his son and daughter-in-law in the niceties of good customer service. Jane started working in the store soon after the birth of her daughter in 1899.

Always aware of the racial divide, they were within limits in their contact with the black majority. But Miss Jane knew many of the customers as fellow workers when she was a hungry, needy throwaway white trash. She was grateful to her husband, but her concern for others was a trait that gained her respect from the black customers and scorn from some of the white ones. It was the store that served as a catalyst, bringing both races together, however limited in contact. It remained a unique spot to meet and chat and find out what was going on. Yet, a distinct racial divide remained, even in the remote country store. Blacks came and went and didn't linger while the whites would sit around the stove and chat away. A perfunctory nod or "yes, sir" was the norm, and that was the extent of most of the contact.

Thus it was that the Hurley General Store was the place to be. Where else would you discuss all the problems or get advice? Churches and schools were segregated, but the store was there for everyone. Divided and subject to the norm of Jim Crow South, it was, nevertheless, a place to gather and get information.

So, today, the big news was the arrival of several official US telegrams addressed to the young men of the county. It was big news and the news of its arrival brought a large crowd of curious young man of both races to the store.

The trip to Hurley's was a mere six-minute walk on the same dusty, unpaved path that had been used since slave days. With his friend Charles, James left for the store, telling his younger brother that his mother should be aware that he would possibly have some mail—mail that would alter completely his plans to head north. But it would be welcome news, even if it meant going to a far-off country to fight. He smiled when he thought of his people's plight and the indignities of Jim Crow. *Now they want our blood spilled over there to fight these Germans! Don't know no Germans—guess we're supposed hate them. I know I never even heard of these people until now.*

He didn't know what the fight was all about. He had heard some of the white men and a few blacks talk about Wilson wanting to beat the Germans. He paid little attention until the United States got involved in April 1917. After that, the talk was more intense. He remembered the other white, elderly gentleman from Greenville saying that soon they would come here to the delta to recruit both black and white boys.

"Just a matter of time, that's all," one old Civil War veteran, Leroy McElroy, replied in response to the tense atmosphere that had prevailed for at least a week. And veteran McElroy was right on target. He recalled how the telegrams came in 1862 when he and two others were recruited to fight for the rebel cause. "Hell, I remember everyone blaming the Yankees for everything. Yet, they spilled the same damn blood we did."

Jane looked up at this frank comment from McElroy. He was a respected old gent who had seen a great deal of blood during the Civil War. A veteran of the Battle of Gettysburg, he was one of the few members of Pickett's Charge who came away unscathed. His experience in the war and the aftermath of occupation by the Union army in Mississippi made him think twice before offering full support the war that Mr. Wilson wanted. Jane, looking at the seventy-three-year-old vet, smiled and poured him an extra cup of coffee. "This is on the house, old Leroy."

He brought a moment of sanity to all the war talk that was ongoing since the telegrams arrived. She walked back to the counter. "I hate to be the bearer of this news, but both the whites and coloreds are going off to war. Don't make sense to me, either, Leroy—no, makes no sense to me," she added as if to emphasize the point.

Shaking her head, she returned to the counter to assist a woman who had gathered a few staples. Adding up the bill, she packaged the bag of potatoes, a stalk of carrots, and a tin can of dry red-kidney beans. "That'll be $1.09, Miss Kelly," she said to the middle-aged woman who was also listening to the chatter around the stove where McElroy and his two old friends, Frank Larson and Johnnie Patton, were sitting. Looking their way, she said, "Mr. McElroy, I do hope this war is quick. I have a sixteen-year-old boy. If it continues, I'm sure his daddy will be upset. Planting season will be here before long and you know how Mr. Crawley—"

Interrupting Agnes Kelly, whose family he knew, he quickly added, "Don't you worry about that, ma'me. Crawley will need as much help as he can get. Your boy is safe for now. Looks like those people in Washington decided on eighteen- to forty-five-year-olds," he added, giving her a reassuring nod.

Forcing a smile, she picked up her bag, adding, "Thank you. I hope you're right," and proceeded out the door.

Leroy felt good that at least she understood that, for the moment, her life would not be disrupted with the prospect of her boy going off to war. He recalled how his own mother those many years before couldn't understand why her family had to send two sons off in a cause she didn't quite get. He remembered her saying, "We got no beef with the Yankees, we don't own slaves, and we're scrapping a living in this god-forsaken land."

Yes, he remembered it well and knew both he and his older brother, Virgil, were lucky ones who returned. *Did it for the South, whatever that meant.* So many didn't return. He just hoped the crop of boys going off from the Crawley land, both white and black, would understand what it was all about. But with wars, it's always the young who sacrifice. This war would be no different. New weapons, new "arts" of war from machine guns, German U-boats, mustard gas, and airplanes hitting cities. It was war, and it got good at killing with the new machines of war.

He knew better than to stay. He still had nightmares from a half-century before thinking of the charge up Cemetery Ridge with Pickett's Charge. He didn't want to stay and see the young men about to get their patriotic duty to a calling they probably less about than he did. He decided to leave before the work crew arrived with the message to pack off for basic training. As he exited the door, he noticed James Hayes walking up the rickety, wooden steps.

"Lord knows what these boys are going to face," Leroy muttered to no one and shaking his head, headed home.

CHAPTER 5

James Hayes arrived with his friend Charles at 4:10 p.m. at Hurley's. Unlike most of the people who had come expecting the worst news that their sons were drafted, James had a different take. He was humming a silent tune and in a good mood. Yet, he quickly remembered not to show too much elation to the crowd of people who had gathered. *Mama always told me to be on guard and not get too loud when in public. She don't want me to end up like my uncle. Acting too brash, she calls it. I owe her that much, but I can't take no bullshit from these crazy, tired folks, both white and black.* Today would be different. He could feel it. He was ready for whatever fate had in store.

Entering the store, he noticed the small contingent of concerned parents were on hand to await the opening of the mail. Many of the older folks, both black and white, couldn't read, so it was the job of Jane Hurley to dispense the news, however grave it may be. The one thing he noticed was how quiet it was inside. Normally a beehive of activity and buzz, it was eerily abnormal to observe how quiet the store, despite the presence of some twelve people, was that afternoon. As he looked about, he saw the usual white guys sitting in the center near the stove while the blacks, as always, were standing about near the door.

James, scanning the familiar faces, knew something was different. He could see the fear in the eyes of the older grandmothers. The parents, eight number, were silent. A few of the young men who were expecting the news were on hand, yet most of them were still working and would remain working until sundown, about 5:30 p.m.

He also knew that old Crawley would do his best to make sure that his best muscle force would not go off to war. James knew he would have to confront him and tell him, whatever ties Warren Crawley had to the local draft board, that he wanted out. Life in the delta, always a challenge, was overwhelming the antsy young man. It was only a matter of time for him to escape this dismal life—even this crazy war. So what if he had to fight in some far-off land? It would be worth the chance. So what if he didn't know or care who the enemy was? It was a meal ticket out. So what if the military was segregated? He would show his pride and skills and get noticed. So, he was so ready—so very ready! Whatever awaited him, it had to be better than this miserable existence. Trying not to look smug lest he create a scene with some of the surly "good old boys," his entry into the store with his friend was uneventful and careful.

Greeting Jane Hurley with a polite nod, he and Charles proceeded to the back corner away from the center stove. If standard protocol was followed, Ms. Jane would give the mail out and ask if anyone needed to have their contents read. If so, she was discreet enough to take the individual, both black and white, to an area and read the contents of the letter from a far-off relative. Today, of course, was different. She knew it, and the assemblage did too. The tension could be cut with a knife. A few of the ladies had handkerchiefs and were dabbing at their eyes. Within a few minutes, Jane Hurley would take center stage and give her performance, like it or not. She was the center of attention and would give the news to her concerned customers. Theater mixed with melodrama was the rule of the day.

Jane began by announcing, "Y'all know that the war is on and that our boys are going off to war."

"We know that, Janey! Just tell us what's in the letter!" shouted one of the landowners, Preston Grey.

"Let her speak," shouted one of the ladies. Getting nods from both men and women, Grey knew he had crossed the line with Southern gentility and kept quiet.

"Okay, okay, sorry, ma'am." Preston sat down and looked to the floor to avoid the smirks on a few faces.

As a big landowner, Grey wanted his gang labor to stay intact. Like his fellow landlord, Warren Crawley, he controlled the type of crops grown on the land, supervised the production, and controlled the marketing and bookkeeping. He was, in a word, a landlord with a vast entrepreneurial empire composed of vassals working for subsistence wages for him. This telegram was not welcomed by him or any of the other landlords who wanted to keep the status quo. And like other rural elites, he wanted to protect his holdings. That meant keeping both black and white on the land. Despite the fact that the draft boards in Mississippi were the domain of whites, many landlords were insecure and afraid to lose

their able-bodied men running off to fight a foreign foe they didn't care about. He knew that anxious white Southern men had claimed that Northern labor agents had come south to lure blacks up north with the prospect of jobs. The Great Migration had already been a social movement that took on a life of its own. Going north meant a better life and an end to the dead-end life of a sharecropper. The letters that James Hayes's family got from his uncle served as a catalyst to lure the most recalcitrant poor blacks to reconsider a complete uprooting of their lives. The informal network of family, friends, and black newspapers was a further incentive to get up and make the move. The prospect of going north and starting over became a major goal of people like James Hayes. The interruption of the US entry into the World War made the trek seemed more plausible to him and instilled concern and even fear from the landlords. Jane Hurley was aware of this dilemma and decided that the assembled throng of antsy homefolk needed some reassurance. The tension in the room was clearly evident. Jane Hurley knew this and asked for everyone to pay attention. She was ready for her big moment!

Jane scanned her audience, like a good actress and began: "The telegram came from the War Department. It lists the following names."

At this point, the room fell eerily quiet. The loud jaybirds interrupted the silence with their loud cackling sound. Jane knew this news would shatter lives and uproot so many families. Although she had no sons, she knew the simple people of the delta would suffer from this action. Like it or not, the news wasn't going to be good. Most of the owners and workers didn't know or care about the far-off conflict in the French trenches. They were proud Southerners and would answer the call of their country. It was the owners who worried most. They had the most to lose of a dying institution of sharecropping, a second-class life imposed in the Jim Crow South.

Losing their best and most reliable workers, they would have to gather a further labor force. So it was people like Preston Grey who had the most to lose in terms of livelihood. The boys called up would go to war and see the world—a totally different world that they knew from the delta. Owners like Grey and James's boss, Warren Crawley, knew that the twentieth century was making the world smaller with the advent of the automobile, the radio and the lure of jobs up north. The demands of the Northern businesses in contracting with the federal government would only increase the migration north. Their way of life that they controlled through the sharecropping system was in jeopardy, and it was just a matter of time before it too would change.

Jane read the names. Groans and gasps from some of the women were augmented by the shaking of heads and cries of, "Oh no, my boy is going." Jane, ever the main act, knew it was her time to speak.

Jane tried to reassure the group that this was merely a call to report to the draft board and that the draftees would have to pass a physical and know how to read and write. She knew that alone would eliminate probably close to 40 percent of the sixteen names she recited.

When Jane read the name *James Hayes*, and looked his way, he smiled and put his head down, not wanting others to see the glee in his face. He was so happy, knowing fully well that he could pass a physical hands down and could read. He had the equivalent of a sixth-grade education. The remorse or guilt leaving his family with a crippled father and sick brother could now be explained that it was a clarion call to fight for his country. He felt good that he could tell his parents that he wasn't leaving voluntarily but had to report to the draft board. James knew that old Crawley would try to interfere with the local draft board. He had connections with the local politicos and would demand to be heard. But James Hayes would be resolute and not give in an inch. If he couldn't get up North and start life, he would fight, in whatever capacity, for his country. He didn't give a damn about the war objectives or the enemy; he just was a young, ambitious, and angry man who wanted out of a miserable life. Going off to war, even if it meant death, would be better than enduring the injustices he had encountered in his young life. Witness to these injustices from the fields where he worked to the local convenience stores and the segregated lifestyle was too troubling for him. He wanted out and tasted the freedom that could come. He was indeed ready to escape and proceeded back to his home knowing that his family would be devastated. *It's my time, and I gots to get out. Ain't no other way. I'm tired of moving out of the way for white people. Tired of the bullshit that comes with this life. Tired of the "Yes, sir, no sir" mentality. Tired of being called boy when I'm bigger, stronger, and smarter than these old bastards! Yeah, I'm ready. There'll be no turning back for me. Hell, if I make it through the tests, I'll show them what I got. But, I gots to get out now. This war may be my answer. Hate to leave, Mama, but please understand. Ain't no other way. Either I stay here and become a miserable old field hand or I get to that damn war. Not even close. I know what to tell the folks. Damn well, I do!*

With his notice in hand, James descended the four wooden steps and walked into the dimming light peering through the cottonwoods. He picked up his pace, smiling and starting to sing one of his favorite hymns, "I'm on My Way." He remembered his pastor, Jesse Atkins, telling the congregation at his church, Zion Baptist, that this hymn was about the Israelites escaping the bondage of slavery in Egypt. He especially enjoyed singing the verse:

> I'm on my way to freedom land
> I'm on my way, praise God,
> I'm on my way.

He at once felt so much better and started singing louder as he got further away from Hurley's General Store. Over and over, he sang the line, "I'm on my way to freedom."

CHAPTER 6

When he arrived home, James's mother greeted him by saying, "So what's this I hear, you going off to war, son!" The look on her stone cold glare demanded a response and James did not let the moment go away.

"Yes, Mama, it sure looks that way."

"Not if I have anything to say about this!" Her voice cracked as she looked at her husband, who had just added a teaspoon of sugar to his coffee and began stirring, hitting the side of the cup loudly. Jeremiah didn't want to respond, knowing that a confrontation with the missus was one he would lose. He let his son—the center of the dispute—do all his bidding. His eldest son, James, came into the shack, letter in hand and ready for the unfolding drama.

James knew he had to stand his ground. A quick glance at his dad and brother, who had his head buried in his hands, allowed James the opening he wanted. "I know you want me to stay here and—"

"Son, I don't want see my boy going off to some crazy place I don't know nothing about to fight some so-called enemy." Lula Mae stared directly at her son James, raising her voice. "Look, your Uncle Moses has put the idea of leaving in your head and heading off to Chicago." She stopped short, going to the stove with two pots simmering and added, "Let's sit. Your dinner will get cold."

"Yes, son." His father got up to retrieve the spoon. He had dropped his teaspoon he was playing with while his wife ranted. Now was the time for him to speak. "Your mom ain't concerned about you wanting to leave. We all know that to be true. This life here is miserable for us, and I want you and your brother to get ahead, but …" Not finishing his thought and looking down, he paused, stirred his coffee after wiping the spoon with his napkin.

"I know you care and I don't want to leave like this, but it's a way out," James noted as his mother motioned to him and his brother to sit, as dinner was ready.

Jeremiah added, "Eat something, everybody. We can talk better on a full tummy, even me."

His father's attempt at humor wasn't going well. Mrs. Hayes had prepared fried chicken, her special batter always a hit, with mashed potatoes and black beans. Her recipe for fried chicken was legendary. She was always asked to donate a portion to the Sunday after-service social held at Zion Baptist once a month. The aroma from the fried chicken was enough to quiet the family. Lula Mae knew comfort food, such as her celebrated chicken, would speak for itself.

Placing the sumptuous spread on the table, she proudly announced, "See if you get this kind of meal wherever you're going!" Yes, comfort foods always seemed to work in difficult situation and crises. This was no exception. She was, after all, a mother and loving parent. A strong woman, she ruled the roost and would have her say. But she was also a mother. She couldn't stay angry and confused; she smiled at her eldest boy, James, and placed a gentle touch to his shoulder as she brought a pitcher of lemonade to the table. Wiping her hands on her plain white apron, she sat at the other end of the wooden table. Picking up a chicken thigh, she began to eat following a quick grace from her husband.

James, sitting next to his brother and his father, gave them both a shy smile, adding, "Things gots to get better. Makes no sense—you going off to this war. It's like this place, this life. Just want you to know that." Jeremiah gave both of his boys a wink. With that, James felt he had to speak up.

"Look, I know you care. But I just can't sit back and do nothing.

Besides, this is from the government! Like you said, Dad, what kind of life is this in this god-forsaken land? I've been wanted to leave but with your accident and …" James didn't want to complete his thought, for all eyes were on him. He bit into a chicken thigh, adding, "Daddy's right, let's eat up."

The family sat down and dug into the dinner that his mom had prepared.

About halfway through the meal, James's father had to get something off his chest. "I spoke to Warren Crawley."

"What about!" James quickly put down his chicken thigh, wiping his mouth with his cloth napkin, demanding, "What does that old man Crawley have to say? He's got no business in my business."

"Now, you just calm down." It was indeed time to speak his mind. "Crawley's been using us black folk and even some of those poor whites from the valley, just to get rich. What do we have? A patch of land and a shack with a chicken coop and a miserable patch of land to grow things. C'mon, is this what we want?"

Nathaniel, his younger brother, always shy and reluctant to speak, decided it was his time to express his opinion. "I don't want James to leave, but he's right. He's right! There's nothing here for him and for us for that matter. I know that you're scared about his going off, maybe over to that war to that country …"

"France." James let out a laugh.

"Okay, France. Wherever you go, if they let you, you'll be up to snuff man." Nathaniel gave his brother a nudge, who returned one to his sibling in kind. His mother, seeing the fraternal bonding, smiled, knowing that little further could be said on either side of the matter.

"As far as I can see, Crawley has no say in the matter." James was pleased to make his point.

"Not at all true, young man." Jeremiah needed to give his son a lesson. "All these damn draft boards are controlled by the local good old white boys, and they send or stop from sending you off. If Crawley wants you to work his land, all he has to do is give your name to the people at the office and tell them you're needed."

"Wait a minute! Wait a minute! Crawley has enough control over us—the land, the work, our life. He's not going to do a damn thing to stop me from at least going up and checking things out." He quickly glanced at his mother, knowing her disdain for cursing at any time. "I don't care how he feels about us—he's just looking out for himself, and we all know that!"

With that statement, James shook his head and looked at his brother, who shouted, "Amen to that!" James tore into another piece of chicken.

The politics of the delta and much of rural America in 1917 was such that local draft boards could exercise much power. The nearest courthouse was in Raymond, just five miles away from the Crawley land. The old courthouse, built in 1857, stood proud during the Civil War and was an example of fine Georgian art with columns. Crawley tried to avoid going there unless absolutely necessary. But it was important for him to get to the Raymond Courthouse, as he knew the local draft board official Johnny Grey had an office on the second floor.

Although Crawley, who was known to put pressure on local politicos to get favors, didn't always succeed. Many disliked his in-your-face attitude and that he felt entitled to get answers right away. He often got his point across and influenced events to benefit him. This situation, however, involved the federal government. Like it or not, he had to deal with the prospect of losing his best field hands. He knew what he had to do, futile as it may turn out. He also knew that other landlords would soon be at Grey's office demanding that he give exemptions to the prospective draftees.

Within a day of the draft notices, Warren Crawley headed straight to the Hinds County Courthouse to see the chair of the local draft board, Johnny Grey. He had told Jeremiah that he would do all possible to get James out of the draft. But Johnny Grey was someone who had run-ins before. He didn't need Crawley breathing down his back and asking for favors. But Grey was ready for any drama about to unfold.

He entered the stately antebellum courthouse in Raymond, thirty miles east of Vicksburg and seventeen miles west of the state capital,

Jackson. The beautiful, Greek revival white courthouse, built from 1857 till 1859, survived the Civil War intact. In 1865, two years after Grant captured Vicksburg and thus control of the Mississippi River, twelve thousand Union troops led by Gen. James McPherson were surprised by a smaller but determined rebel force of four thousand Confederate troops. The attack, like most of the encounters, large and small during the four-year war was bloody, resulting in one thousand dead. The courthouse, just a few years old, was used as a hospital. In an age that saw brother fighting brother, the courthouse stayed intact as it addressed the wounded and had a special place in Mississippi history. A half century later, it stood as a proud reminder in the center of the small town.

But it was now 1917, and President Wilson got the Congress to pass the draft bill. For Crawley, the memories of the now far-off war that divided the nation were not in mind. Nor was the history of the majestic courthouse. As a businessman, he was concerned in keeping his labor pool intact. The telegrams that Jane Hurley gave to the prospective draftees demanded immediate action to salvage his status quo. He looked up at the courthouse, giving a sigh, and ascended to the second floor.

Close to retirement and a very lethargic, chronic cougher due to his addiction to strong, pure Camel cigarettes, Johnny Grey knew it just a matter of time before Crawley and the other landlords would be breaking down his second-floor office door above the courthouse. Grey, like most of the South in the early 1900s, was a Democratic-appointed political hack beholden to the white establishment in the delta.

Grey didn't like changes, as evident from the piles of paper on his desk. An ashtray loaded with cigarettes butts with the added constant smell of smoke greeted anyone who dared venture into his inner sanctum. Part of the old order of Southern Democrats whose power in the delta was evident whenever a job favor was asked. He liked his cushy, laid-back job. He was a slacker that no one paid much attention to save for an occasional favor. Crawley's presence at his office, not unexpected, was nevertheless a necessary burden for Grey. He was given a warning that landlords, like Crawley, would be coming as soon as the telegrams arrived at Hurley's General Store.

Entering into the messy, smoky, and smelly environment, Crawley, shaking hands and exchanging pleasantries with Grey, the political hack and product of the old, staid Jim Crow establishment in the delta, decided to come right to the point.

"You know the draft notices are going to do damage to all of us by taking my best …" Crawley was in no mood to for an explanation from his old friend, Johnny Grey.

Grey, extinguishing his fifth cigarette of the morning, rose up and walked over to his friend. Although sympathetic to Crawley, he had his orders from the feds. He had to fill the quota as demanded by the feds and he proceeded to explain the quota system to Crawley.

"I don't give a damn about no Germans. Hell, most of my darkies and whites don't either. They don't even know how to get the hell of this county, let alone the state and country. This will set back my orders, and it will disrupt our economy." Crawley, looking at Grey, waited for an answer that he hoped would ameliorate his personal crisis.

"No can do, Warren."

"Why not? Can't you tell the board and the officials in Jackson that we can't spare any of these men?" Clearly agitated, Warren Crawley, used to being in charge, was being challenged now by forces beyond his reach. Sensing the tension arising, Johnny Grey, not known to be a compassionate sort, walked over to his friend, adding, "You'll have to use whatever labor pool you can get. Maybe the boys in Jackson will send a chain gang …"

"Oh, hell no, Johnny. Those no-good bastards will only try to escape. We'll have more problems than you can ever imagine. And prison guards. Have to feed them too! On private land, we landlords wouldn't stand for it." Grey went back to his desk, taking off his glasses and looking over a document on his desk. A bottle of Jack Daniels in his front right desk was conveniently covered by a cloth napkin. Looking at the unopened fifth of alcohol he thought, *I'll get to you once I finish with this cranky old bastard Crawley*. Looking up and forcing a smile, he added, "I can only say this one more time. I got my order and the list of men—"

"Bullshit!" Crawley interrupted, adding, "You're just looking out for yourself."

That bottle is going to get my attention sooner than later. Grey composed himself and knew it was time to give Crawley a history lesson.

"Sorry, Warren, I know some of these boys can't even write their name. Not all of them are going to be shipped off to fight this Kaiser or whatever. But I've played with the numbers that the draft board wants from the county and came up with this list. This is from the goddamn feds. The same list Jane Hurley read at the store and …" Johnny Grey sat at his desk looking down at the myriad papers on his desk. He hoped that the encounter with Crawley was coming to a close, knowing little could be accomplish by a back-and-forth confrontation.

"Yeah, I'm sorry too! Sorry that they're destroying my labor pool. Sorry that our way of life here in the delta is being messed up by the government. I know you're not personally responsible, but I got to get through this mess. It doesn't add up for me, that's all I'm saying." Warren turned, heading for the door. Hitting his broad brim hat forcefully on his left thigh, he added, "All right, Johnny, there's not much more to say." The expression on Grey's face clearly was one of relief despite the agitation he experienced with Crawley.

As he was exiting the open door, Grey felt the need to reassure his old buddy. "I wanted to be up front with you but damn—I'm trying, it just that …"

"I know you got your orders," Crawley shouted as he left. *I hope to Christ most don't pass the physical. I'm loyal to the country up to a point, but this is not good. Not good for me, my land, the delta, and our way of life.*

Leaving the county courthouse, he caught sight of Wendell Pickens, another large landowner in the county. He nodded to Pickens, who returned the pleasantry. Sensing his exasperation, Pickens looked up at the courthouse and asked, "Any luck with that old chain-smoking fool, Grey?"

The description brought a smile to the face of Warren Crawley, who responded, "Hell no! Maybe you can do better with that stubborn old codger. You're here for the same reason, I reckon?" Crawley added.

"Yes sir. I'll give it my best, but I know it's a shot in the dark dealing with that fool—he'll do exactly what the state says and not change anything to help us out. We need to stick together and appeal to Jackson and the governor, if need be." Pickens was a level-headed, less prone to outbursts than Crawley, and would be the person who officials could work with when necessary.

"Good luck with Johnny Grey. Got to get back to the house and see if any other surprises are in store for us. You take care, you hear," Crawley tipped his hat and got into his Model T.

"Will do, will do. Y'all remember me to the missus too." And with that he turned and headed to the same office that Warren Crawley had just exited.

Given the news he just received from Johnny Grey at the Raymond Courthouse, Crawley got into his vehicle and took a deep breath. He had tried the art of persuasion to no avail. *Damn, if I have to—I'll contract out with the county and get a chain gang on my land. As long as I can get my products out, I'll be okay. But this isn't good for any of us.*

CHAPTER 7

"You have to be at the draft board in Raymond by nine a.m. for a physical."

Lula Mae knew her son couldn't contain his excitement at the prospect of leaving his tough life. Despite her reticence at the thought of losing her eldest child in some far-off and strange land in a conflict she still didn't understand, she had come to terms with it all. Orders were orders, and like any good mother, she was aware of importance of showing up on time. Yet she had a restless night once the day of reckoning arrived. She and her husband knew there would be one less mouth to feed, but at what price? It was her eldest who literally carried the water for the family. She felt she could hold onto him for a year or two before he ran off to Chicago or got married, but this order was not welcomed. The main concern for her son was that, like thousands of other young Americans called up for service, they would venture into a foreign terrain rife with deadly consequences. Rumors had come even to the delta of the Germans' atrocities from the sinking of the Lusitania in 1915 to the use of mustard gas that suffocated the victim and drowned his lungs. As a mother, she was indeed scared. For her son, it was altogether different.

James had mixed feelings too. He was eager to leave the bleak, dismal life in the delta. Yet he was torn by the fact that he would leave a sick brother and father. Still, he had his whole life ahead of him. There would be no turning back. The eldest son of Lula Mae and Jeremiah was very ready to leave the nest and head out and begin a life. Even if that meant going into combat and risk getting killed, it would get him out of the delta. *Anything is better than this miserable life!*

He was dressed and cleaned up and ready to walk the three-mile trek along the dusty road to the courthouse where the local doctor, hired by the War Department, would conduct the physical exam, a first step in the process of going off to basic training. He was ready for any eventuality.

Outside, it was a dreary day—damp and a wisp of fall that creeps slowly up on you. The cool air, augmented by a brisk wind, made the walk to the courthouse more challenging for the young man intent on getting out of this bleak life. *Even if they don't take me, I'm going to get out of here soon,* James thought as he took one last look in the cracked mirror. He liked what he saw—clean shaven, close-cropped hair, and his Sunday white shirt and black slacks.

The damp air, coupled with the strong wind, would indeed challenge anyone venturing out and walking any long distance. *I don't care if it's below zero. I'm heading to that old courthouse and taking care of business!*

Motivated and eager, James got ready for the trek to Raymond Courthouse, where a local doctor hired by the War Department would check all county draftees and determine if they were fit for basic training in far-off Kansas at Fort Riley's Camp Funston. *Hell, I'm in good shape. Never been to a dentist, but my teeth is good and my body is sound.* James was euphoric, and despite the threat of rain on the damp, dark day, he was ready for his debut. Deep inside, he knew today would be important for him. Regardless of how the physical would turn out, he was very determined to get on with his life. Like most young men coming of age, he was curious.

He had been only once to the courthouse with his father to check on a small inheritance obtained from an elderly spinster aunt, Julia Springer. He remembered climbing up to the second-floor office of the attorney, who had a check for his dad. It amounted to $352 after state taxes. For his father, it was a windfall, and he was able to purchase some items sorely needed—a new pot-belly stove for his wife plus a stop at Hurley's to buy his wife a new dress and matching blue bonnet for church. The rest he put in the bank and left a small account for a rainy day. James's reflection of that day at the courthouse didn't sit well with him. The attorney in charge was brusque and made them wait well over an hour past the appointed hour while he attended to other "matters." This event and the fact that he charged his dad for his services further eroded James's confidence in the mattes of state when black folk were concerned. He hated the system and was determined to get out. If this was his meal ticket out, however dangerous, he was willing to take the chance.

Today, however, would be different. He wouldn't let any short-sighted bigots stand in his way to break loose and get out of this miserable existence. He wouldn't tolerate the injustice of being a second-class citizen any longer. With mixed emotions, he bid adieu to his mom and set out for the courthouse, telling her that he wouldn't be too long. As he exited the screen door that had seen better days with holes that allowed flies and mosquitoes easy access to their home, he looked back. His mom, a smile on her face, had come to terms with her son's desire to leave.

She turned to her husband, again reiterating his date with destiny, adding, "I hope he does pass all the tests and makes us proud."

Jeremiah, always a man of few words, merely added, "Whatever he does, it'll be all right."

The trip to the courthouse took just thirty minutes by foot. The road, unpaved and dusty, was the only connection with the outside world from the small patch of land he called home. The road was not in the best condition, especially on a rainy day. Intermittent puddles and loose rocks made one navigate carefully lest one soil whatever one had worn that day.

Despite the puddles and rocks, James picked up his pace. Within a few minutes, he recognized a friend of his mother's, Grace Purdey, walking in the opposite direction. Mrs. Purdey had seen hard times over her sixty-seven years—a widow, she had a son a few years older than James who was in state prison on trumped-up charges of stealing from a gin joint. The fact that he was accused was enough for a conviction despite his pleas to the court that he wasn't anywhere in the area. The actual culprit was a white kid and nephew of the sheriff. The owner knew who committed the crime but was told to say nothing until "arrangements could be met." They charged Grace Purdey's son, Henry, with the crime. The owner, Jeff White, was told he wouldn't get his liquor license renewed if the sheriff's nephew, Frank Buell, was charged. "That was the way it was done," White was told. Yet, an innocent black man would be unjustly convicted in Jim Crow Mississippi. The threats to the club owner notwithstanding, the system protected their own.

With such a threat from local law enforcement official, a scapegoat was needed. Henry Purdey, on his way home from a job site, was the perfect fall guy. Young, black, and no connection to the town, he was taken into custody. He lived outside the hamlet of Edwards some five miles west.

It was his word against the timid owner of the bar, and forced to lie under oath, the owner, Jeff White, capitulated and said it was Henry. White's conscience bothered him to the point where he took to the bottle. Within a year, he was placed in a sanitarium and his business collapsed. To protect a felon, two lives—Henry Purdey and Jeff White's—were ruined. But the young nephew of the sheriff, Frank Buell, thanks to his uncle, was never indicted. That was indeed the way the system worked.

With no credible alibi, Henry Purdey was found guilty by an all-white male jury. The jury was out just twenty-two minutes! Placed on a chain gang for two years, he tried to escape within a few months. With an aborted attempt to break free, he was shot at and luckily, the officer missed, despite the rifle aimed at him. Nevertheless, he was given an additional two years to his sentence, taken off the chain gang, and put in state prison. Henry, always a source of income for his mother, was no longer there for her. Grace Purdey got by with ironing and cleaning, and today, as James caught sight of her, she was on her way to home of Warren Crawley. One of many domestics, she cleaned, cooked, and occasionally watched over Crawley's granddaughter, Alice.

"Good morning, Ms. Grace." James tipped his wide-brim hat, smiling at the elderly woman.

"Why James, you dressed like it's for church, but today's only Wednesday."

"Yes, ma'am, but I'm my way to the courthouse …"

"Oh, no, you be careful, you didn't …"

"No, no, it's not nothing like that. I didn't do nothing. I got a draft notice and got to report." James gave her a big smile.

Grace Purdey, never one to hold back, added, "Still, you be careful, boy—you hear? I know about this draft thing. A few of the boys got a notice from Ms. Jane Hurley's."

"Yes, I'm one of them. I don't know what's up except that I may be off to this war."

With that, Ms. Grace gently touched his arm, "You be careful. Your mama will be worried."

"I know. I know." James turned and waved at the lady who he knew from church and always had something nice to say about his mom. James thought of Miss Grace, as she was known, and felt sorry for what life had dealt her. Her history of hard life and the unfairness to her son reinforced young James's determination to get out. He knew that her son, once out, would have a criminal record and would always be suspect if any wrongdoing took place. He felt sorry for Henry and Miss Grace. *It ain't gonna happen to me. Not me. Not me!*

Picking up a dry twig, he repeatedly hit his left thigh with it and began humming one of his favorite hymns. Keeping a steady rhythm, he improvised and ad libbed whatever came into his head. This is what he did when he wanted to let the world go away momentarily and daydream a bit. *Someday, I'll make some music that others will enjoy.* As he picked up his pace, he didn't look back and was ready to face what eventuality awaited him. The past was behind him; it was a new day. *Before another sun rises, I will put this life behind me. My family will understand; they have no choice.*

James was coming to terms with himself and knew it was his hour. The tragic and horrific events of World War I catapulted the world into a maelstrom of death and suffering beyond anyone's imagination. With submarine warfare, poison gas, machine guns, and airplanes used, it was truly a modern and catastrophic event. It would also witness many civilian deaths, unlike previous conflicts. Regardless of the possibility of becoming a casualty, James would take up the challenge. *It can't get much worse than this wretched life!*

For James, this trek to the courthouse was to become a seminal event in his life. He could feel it in his bones. He knew that that the notice a few weeks earlier on October 7 was indeed a wake-up call for him. No longer would he be subject to the indignities of a boss who cared only about profit. No longer would he have to be silent for his dad and brother. No longer would he be treated as a second-class citizens without speaking up. His continued silence was testament to his mom's concern, and he kept things inside him. He didn't like it. No longer would he have to! He knew the dreary life in the delta would ultimately overwhelm him and make him a bitter person. He was too strong both mentally and physically to capitulate to the indignities perpetrated by Jim Crow. He would have none of this! He was ready for any eventuality in his life. He had to get out. He knew it. His family knew it too.

He looked back at the road. He smiled and looked ahead and let out an audible sigh. Looking around, he saw an antsy jaybird in a cottonwood tree. He looked up at it and smiled. He took a deep breath. He stopped in his tracks and looked at the determined jaybird who began to sing. *Maybe mating season! Lucky bird! Like him, I'll be free to go about, to sing. To do anything and go anywhere! You're lucky, jaybird. No one will stop you from your singing. You can go and do what you want. Such a lucky bird. Soon, I hope I have that kind of freedom. Soon, very soon!* A smile overcame him as James took in the moment. Despite his situation, there was a beauty to the land in the stillness of the early morning. The smells of the wild flowers, the singing of the birds, and the bonding with nature all had an effect on him. The stillness was only interrupted by the occasional serenade of today's jaybird. The beauty of the morning rays filtering through the assorted cottonwoods, weeping willows, and dogwood trees. There was a stillness and peace on a rural road yet to be claimed by the automobile and paved roads. And for one young, restless, and ambitious young man born of these lands, it was suddenly a place to absorb and appreciate. Where was he going? He didn't know, nor did anyone. Events would change his life as they would countless others. But the land, along with the smells, songs of nature's creatures, and beauty of it all were his today. No one would get in the way. Like that proud jaybird, he too would set out and make something of his life. He would make his mark and be heard. He knew not where he was heading, but he was so ready.

He cast the twig he was hitting the side of his left thigh with onto the road. The singing jaybird's serenade got fainter and fainter as he put more pep into his step. It would indeed be his day.

His pace picked up further, almost to a jog. His Sunday best clothes should make a favorable impression, he thought. His black shoes were shined. His mom had made sure his white shirt was ironed and his black slacks as well. Yes, his Sunday best. He looked about. He didn't have a clue what would happen to him. Yet he knew deep down in his gut that momentous changes were about to occur. He could indeed feel it deep down in his gut. Confidence overtook him. He had always faced up to challenges. He never backed down from challenges since he was a kid. But today was different. It had to be. These were different challenges that he had absolutely no control over. New challenges! So what!

Challenges might await him from basic training to learning what this war was all about. He could possibly get injured in a conflict he didn't know anything about and travel to a foreign land with little in common. Different language, different food, different religion, and different customs. He shook his head and brushed his hand as if to cast aside all doubt.

All that didn't matter right now. All he cared about was to getting out of this damn delta and starting his life. He was looking ahead. He was ready. He started humming again. He thought of his new friend, the jaybird. He too would be free, like the proud, loud jaybird. He wouldn't have to wait long.

CHAPTER 8

A reality check awaited young James Hayes as he ascended up to the same second floor that his boss, Warren Crawley, had gone to just a week before, trying to avoid his help from getting into the world war. A lot of buzz about the war brought the would-be recruits to the Raymond Courthouse. The black recruits were directed to a small room on the second floor, while the white recruits were assigned to the ground floor with two doctors present. After the white recruits were interviewed and examined, the doctors assigned from the War Department would attend to the black recruits. Like everything in the delta, the blacks were regulated to a second-tier position.

James caught sight of his friend Charles Atwood as he climbed the stairs to the second floor. Already eleven men were standing around a small office with a wooden desk and single chair. The sign "Colored Draftees" was on the door. No one was inside, as the officials from the War Department from the doctor assigned to the two fed agents were attending to the nine white draftees downstairs in more spacious and comfortable surroundings.

James approached Charles, shaking hands, announcing, "I see you made it here." James examined the expression on his friend's face. It was one of anxiety, fear, and uncertainty.

"I don't want to go to no war, unlike you. I don't like working for that bastard Crawley, but I—"

James quickly interjected, "Look, Charles, I know how you feel with the baby and all. Just take it easy." Towering over his diminutive friend, the six-foot-one James Hayes quickly added, "You have possible conditions that might stop you from going into the war?" James tried hard to console his friend, knowing that the odds of getting rejected by the draft board were not good.

"I do have flat feet!" he said, letting out a laugh.

James, looking at his friend, said, "Well, there you go. Just tell them the truth about the baby and all too."

The wait to finish with the white draftees took two hours. Finally, the doctor and the two federal officials ascended the stairs with the omnipresent Mr. Grey. Entering into the small space allocated for blacks, Grey, apparently tired from his encounter with the white draftees, said, "Stay in the hallway. I'll call your name and you'll come in to see the doc. Understood?" Grey didn't expect an answer, but the nods from the nervous group made it perfectly clear that Grey, despite the presence of federal officials, was in charge.

James waited and waited. As with the others, it seemed to take forever. Within thirty minutes, the first draftee was called in, and then James's name was announced. Seeing the well-dressed, smiling prospective recruit, the doctor and assistant asked James to disrobe down to his underwear behind a white screen. Obligingly, James was ready for whatever examination awaited him. The doctor, a Midwesterner without racial baggage, was Michael Foley of Chicago.

Dr. Foley affixed his stethoscope and proceeded to ask James to breathe in deeply. Finding no evidence of tuberculosis, he then checked his heart rate and blood pressure. He then asked him to open his mouth, checking his teeth and upper jaw.

"Have you ever been to a dentist?" the doctor inquired of James.

Told not to lie under any circumstances, James replied, "No, sir, can't say that I have."

"Remarkable! Your teeth are clean and pristine."

"Huh," James said, looking up at the doctor. "You mean I'm okay."

"Yes, young man, in top shape. Wish I could say the same for the other recruits both downstairs and here. The army should welcome the likes of you, young man."

James at once felt euphoric and wanted to shout out in joy. "Do you mean I can go and do my job in the army?"

The doctor, noticing the expression on James's face, added, "We do have to check your vision and make sure you see well."

"I think I'll be okay; I shoot squirrel, rabbit, and possum with no trouble, sir!" James wanted to add whatever he could to get a thorough clean bill of health. The doctor smiled, knowing that the young man was eager to get a clean bill of health.

"I don't doubt that. You living in this rural area. I'm sure you have to fend yourself at times." The doctor proceeded to pull down the eye chart.

"Young man, do you know the alphabet?" Dr. Foley was amazed at the recruits who failed this part of the test due to systematic illiteracy in both the black and white recruits.

"Yes, sir. I can read a bit, too."

At this point, Dr. Foley asked the anxious young man how far down the scale he could read the letters clearly.

"I can see all the way to the end line." James proudly recited the letters in exact formation: E-P-O-R-Q-S-V.

"Excellent, young man. Excellent." Foley proceeded to write his findings on the form each of the recruits was asked to sign.

"You're finished here. You now need to go to the next room. They have information for recruits like you as to where you'll get basic. Good luck! You do the army good, very good."

The doctor reached out and shook James's hand. This kind expression was unusual in the delta for a black and white man to show some bonding. The doctor, just out of residency at Chicago Cook County, had patients from this area that migrated north and could feel the hesitancy of the delta newcomers who encountered him at the emergency room in the large urban setting. He volunteered to come down to the delta to help the War Department, once a call was made. Told to be careful as a "Yankee in the heart of the Deep South," his reception by the local officials, like Preston Grey, had been lukewarm. He represented the federal government and was paid by the War Department. Even the conservative, reactionary residents knew that he and others would hold sway. Despite their misgivings about him, he fulfilled his job without any major incident. Yet the simple bond between him and the likes of James Hayes raised eyebrows. For James Hayes, it was indeed a wake-up call. He was ready to move on the next room and sign up!

The adjoining room consisted of a large desk with two local officials. The reception James would receive brought him back to earth. The local officials had kept the black recruits waiting up to two hours. When his name was called, James, along with his friend Charles Atwood and several other black recruits, had remained standing while the white recruits had seats in an adjoining room. Only after the white recruits were attended to did the reluctant local officials, headed by Grey, start giving them notice. James was second to be called.

The person sitting at the desk and looking up at him was a middle-age, overweight local politico named Jeff Hastings. His unkempt hair and large hands complemented a large head with bulging blue, bloodshot eyes. He looked to James like a person who needed a good night's sleep and a bath. His striped, wrinkled shirt had seen better days, as evident in the coffee stains on his left sleeve. James was a keen observer and knew the person he would now confront would determine his fate. It was as simple as that. Regardless of what the doctor recommended, it was up to these local draft boards, all lily white and part of the political patronage that was so pervasive in the South. Yes, it was now decision time. James was determined to stand his ground, ready for any eventuality.

Nervously standing before him, James noticed that Hastings gave him no eye contact and casually remarked, "Boy, you've been recruited to basic training up in Camp Funston in Kansas. You'll be leaving in a week. Here. Take these papers and make sure you don't lose them. You understand, boy?" *Wow! Just like that, I'm in. I'm in!* James found it hard to contain his glee.

James looked down at his command and his heart pounded. He

wanted to say something. He wanted to tell this obese, rumpled local exactly what he felt. The way in which he, along with the other blacks, had to wait, standing until he and others attended to the white applicants in the adjacent room that served as a courtroom replete with chairs and restrooms. He resented the fact that he had to stand, wait and not be given the dignity of a face-to-face contact. He hated this system and wished he could shout out at the top of his lungs how much he hated everything associated with this life.

He decided he would just remain standing until the surly, pencil-pushing SOB looked up. He hated the manner in which he was being dealt. How unlike the doctor! James was a realist and knew that being drafted didn't mean he wouldn't be the subject of further racist and discriminatory practices. But he wanted to take the chance. It couldn't get any worse than being in the delta.

He took a deep breath and swallowed hard, realizing what could transpire if he said something deemed inappropriate, and merely responded, "Yes, sir" when asked questions. No handshake, no thank yous followed. It was the delta after all, and he was supposed to know his place. But like his great-uncle who had been lynched for speaking the truth and demanding justice, James felt victorious. Like the jaybird, he was ready to fly, to sing, to let the world know that he was someone and something. He had overcome the indignities for too long. Now, although knowing that life would be tough and an uncertain future awaited him, he stepped out of the office smiling.

Descending the stairs, he was met by Charles. James was clearly surprised to see that Charles had already apparently concluded his appointment with the board. Moreover, James didn't see him in the assignment room with the other black recruits. As he glanced at his friend, it was clear that Charles had indeed accomplished what he set out to do. He saw his friend James and smiled broadly. It was one of those smiles suggesting that something good had transpired. A certain mischievous smile, no doubt, which made James all the more curious.

He went up to his friend, saying, "I didn't see you in the second room. The one with the locals telling us where to report. I—"

Charles couldn't contain his glee. "I didn't pass the physical. I did tell that nice doctor that I had a wife and kid on the way. He said my teeth were bad. Not bad enough that would stop me from entering the war. But then he checked my eyes. You know what that thing hanging."

James laughed aloud. "You mean the eye chart with all those lines."

"Exactly. I didn't cheat at all. I couldn't see past the second line too good. I tried to read the letters from the second or third line but had trouble. You know how it is; I'm always tripping over something on the job or the road." This comment brought a smile on James's face, and Charles, excited that he wouldn't have to abandon his wife quickly, added, "Anyway, that doc said that my eyesight wasn't up to snuff and he failed me on the physical!" With that, he high fived his friend, knowing that he wouldn't have to abandon his wife and go off to war.

Looking at James, he added, "I know when they took one look at you, they wanted you!"

James Hayes let out a loud laugh, adding, "I guess we both got what we wanted. Yep, they passed me. Just didn't like all the waiting to get past the white boys. But it's good! You gets to stay with your wife while I gets the hell out of this Goddamn place."

With that said, it was indeed time to get home and convey the news to the family. They proceeded out the door, eager to get on their way.

"C'mon, buddy, let's shove off and tell all this to the folks. Mine won't be all that upset with it, but I know your old lady will." Charles Atwood kept looking at James, waiting for a reaction.

James, shaking his head, stopped walking and to make the point come home, pointed his index finger at his friend, announcing, "But I'm getting out of this hell, Charles. I'm getting out, even if it means getting my ass shot off!"

With that, both Charles and James continued out on a path that would lead one back to his meager existence while the other faced an uncertain fate. The unpaved road that had seen so much history from slave times to the Civil War now in the early twentieth century had indeed changed little. For James Hayes, history was about to jolt his senses and introduce him to a world beyond all those wild dreams.

For now, he had to deal with his family. Alongside his friend, he felt a tinge of sadness and regret at leaving his roots. But this was a seminal moment in his life. He could feel it deep down inside. Even Charles sensed it when he looked at his friend.

True, they would go separate ways. Yet, both got what they set out to do. James began humming, thinking of the loud jaybird and imagining the angel in white coming down to escort him to a place where he would be welcomed. His confidence, never in doubt, was restored when the supportive doctor remarked, "You're the best recruit I've seen. And I've been throughout the South from Tennessee and now here in Mississippi. The army would do well with the likes of you." That sealed the deal for him; deep inside James Hayes knew not what awaited him, but unlike his friend Charles, who was bound to the land and would probably remain, he was eager to spread his wings.

As they walked the same dusty road that James had seen the jaybird earlier, he looked up occasionally to see if the old bird was there. Would he still sing to him again? But it was not to be. Charles could hardly contain himself and was smiling and looking at James like he had just won a ball game or caught the largest catfish in the county. They were old buddies who respected each other. James felt a tinge of sadness for Charles. Despite the good news of not going off, he knew that Charles and his brother would be part of the ever-continuing legacy of sharecropping. They were tied to the land, and it would be so hard to escape. For the moment, however, he and Charles got what they wanted, and it was now time to convey the news to their loved ones. For Charles, it would be easy. He would continue to work the Crawley land, till the soil, assist his wife, and be the provider he was destined to be. There was indeed no escape for him with a child on the way.

James's fate would be entirely different. Circumstances of war would ultimately determine what course in life he would take. Although he didn't see the jaybird, he knew that his future would not be in the delta. It couldn't be. He had the initiative, determination, and resolve to make something of his life. He began humming, and Charles joined in too.

They caught up with Jimmie Ray Owens, a white sharecropper

who, like them, had to report to the draft board. Ray was a hard worker and got along well with his black contemporaries. Given the status of the Jim Crow South, he stayed clear of being too friendly to the black coworkers. Yet at times, he and James had to bond whenever the bales were loaded, and Jimmie Ray respected James for his strength and tenacity.

Seeing his coworkers, Jimmie Ray nodded, adding, "They got me. Got to report next week. Guess we'll be in separate units and different places for basics ..." Jimmie Ray gave James a smile, adding, "You're the best worker old Crawley has. He'll be pissed to see you go, but I'm glad you got over."

James, realizing his elusive coworker was trying to show him the respect he desired, said, "Thanks, Jimmie Ray, you take care, you hear. And you're right about what you said about old Crawley and right about the crap about not allowing us colored soldiers to show them what we got." Jimmie Ray reached out his hand and shook hands with James.

"You're right," James added. "The colored troops have to go up to Kansas." He repeated, "Kansas, don't even know where that is."

"Kansas, wow," Jimmie Ray said, looking at both James and Charles. "Well, it's gonna be quite a trip."

With that, he again nodded to them and proceeded to move on. James wondered where the white recruits would travel to, but he had other issues on his mind. Life in the delta was dictated by race. This encounter showed how men of same age and fears would be beholden to the powers that controlled their lives. They could have been teammates on an impromptu baseball team, hanging out, going to music halls, swapping stories about who had the best poker hand, and looking out for each other. But this was the delta. They led separate lives. The war was just an interruption.

The Wilson administration had given a lot of latitude to the local draft boards, and many of the local politicos made sure that their sons and friends were not drafted. They claimed they were too young or too old to serve. In many counties married men with dependents easily earned exemption while in Hinds County both poor white and black with children but no ties to the political machine would be subject to the draft. Jimmie Ray was one of those poor whites who didn't have any connections to the courthouse crowd. Like James Hayes, he too would be given his induction notice to report for basic training. Jimmie Ray gave Charles and James a big wave and proceeded alone down the dusty road, looking back and smiling at them. He kicked up the dust from the unpaved rural road, a symbolic gesture to show his disdain for the entire procedure he had just endured.

"Guess it's gonna be interesting," James said to Charles.

Charles looked up at his newly inducted friend, remarking, "What'cha talking about?"

"Well, look at it this way. You failed the test and you're glad, right?" James couldn't resist getting the point across.

"Yeah."

Charles had a puzzled look as James went on to explain, "Well, they're taking us poor coloreds and these white boys too. But if you have a daddy or uncle or cousin or friends on the board, you could get off but not if you don't have some clout. You see, Jimmie Ray is like us. He don't know anybody, has to work hard in the field, and couldn't get out of this war."

Charles couldn't resist asking, "So what you're saying is that if you and Jimmie Ray wanted to get out of the draft, you could?"

"Yep, and I bet old Crawley's boys won't be going either. Think about it." With that James gave his friend a nudge, and they continued on their way.

The exchange with Jimmie Ray got him to think about injustice—injustice not just based on race but also on income. Jimmie Ray's family was beset by a series of calamites. His mom died when he was just four, and his alcoholic father was in and out of jail and never around—a real deadbeat dad before that term came into prominence. His Aunt Molly tried her best to raise him and his sister but was obese and afflicted with diabetes and died before forty. At fourteen, he was on his own. Jimmie had no choice but to work from age seven. He was an example of the poor, white underclass. He bonded, whenever possible, with his black friend James Hayes, knowing fully well that he too had to be careful. The draft brought these issues of race, economic inequality, and political patronage to a head. Despite their limited education, James, Jimmie Ray, and Charles knew they were pawns in the drama about to unfold.

What James, Charles, and Jimmie Ray experienced was not uncommon in the rural South once the draft was implemented in late 1917. Rural white elites like Grey implemented the draft to protect their sons as well as some of their black workers. James could have faked the eye test or faked illiteracy like many were told to do. But he chose not to, given his desire to escape the indignities of life in the delta.

Reality set in as James approached his home. He prepared to tell his parents that he would be leaving. They would understand. Yet, a certain amount of guilt set in, and his humming stopped, along with the daydreams of the jaybird and the angel. He felt guilty about the fact that his family, although one less mouth to feed, would still be saddled with the indignities of a staid, monotonous life that had little or no advancement. He thought of his dad and his mom and knew they would not only be prepared for his leaving but also expected it. *Just a matter of time, that's all. Like Uncle Moses, I'm getting out.* Nothing would stand in his way now. He walked into his house, holding the paper that would start it all. His mother took one look at him, and smiling, she knew what he was about to tell her.

CHAPTER 9

The train trip due north to Kansas would be James Hayes's first trip outside his provisional world of the delta. In fact, it would be his first time on a train. It had been hard to saying goodbye to his family. It was especially challenging for him to part from the family that was so dependent upon him. Surprisingly, his family stood firm, offering only the best wishes for him and the other seven black men from his area. A special service was held at Zion Baptist for the eight black recruits who were to go off to basic training.

At the Sunday service prior to his Tuesday leaving date, James was asked to sing a solo to the congregation. "Pastor Atkins asked what would be a good song for me and the others. I immediately told him, 'How Great Thy Art.' From the expression on the reverend's face, I knew I made the right choice."

The small but vibrant choir would back him up, and he made sure that the hymn he selected would impact upon the congregation. "How Great Thou Art!" A hymn that was redemptive in nature and an expression of one's faith, putting one's hope in the hands of God. It was so appropriate that James's selection would be this hymn. It spoke to the need to move on, the need to sustain one's faith in spite of the unforeseen. The passages to nature from the breeze in the trees to the songs of the bird made for a joyful chorus to the nervous congregants. The plain, white, wooden church whose steeple rose to sixty feet had been cleaned for the Sunday service. Three plain, triangular-shaped windows on each side plus the eight pews on each side could accommodate seventy to eighty people. On an average Sunday, the Southern Baptist black church attracted fifty or so people. Today, however, every pew was filled. People knew it was a special day. Mothers got their sons to attend, knowing that a portion of the service would pray for the well-being of the eight recruits.

The pulpit was located in the center with a baptismal font in back, behind which rose a large wooden, black cross. To describe the church, one would say it was a simple yet elegant country church. It was a place to worship, bond, and trade stories as well as a venue to exchange the events not only of the delta but also of the greater world.

Today, a spread of flowers was donated by the local undertaker who just buried an elderly congregant, Tobey Madson two days earlier in the adjacent cemetery to the left of the church. Tobey's family was present, and at the suggestion of the undertaker, Thomas Burney, they agreed to grace the pulpit with the flowers. It all looked so nice! The entire setting was indeed set for a special event. And now it was time for James Hayes to take front and center and allow the congregation to hear his gifted voice.

Nodding at the pastor first and then the congregation, James Hayes was ready to shine. His voice soared like never before. The chorus, backing him up for a great sendoff with the other seven, was most inspiring. Soon people were up on their feet. Clapping in unison, smiling, and moving to the beat, it made a most impressive sight. By the third verse, everyone had joined in a triumphant sendoff for their honored young men. James's basso profundo voice had clearly captivated all—from the older ladies in their best dresses and hats to the men in their suits and ties. The younger girls swooned looking at the handsome singer, and no doubt, some of them despite the religious nature of the event thought of other things! These were the salt of the earth people who toiled long and hard and had a history of repression yet maintained a strong faith in the Almighty. Here, in the house of the Lord, they were equal and not subject to the hardships of life.

One of the lady attendees to the service, which was dedicated to "our brothers going off to fight," remarked, "That Hayes boy can sure sing. He needs to get into some band. Perhaps the army will give him a job there. Lord knows they're gonna treat them bad. Lord only knows."

Now, he was heading due north along the Mississippi, passing Memphis and cities in Arkansas, such as Jonesboro, and into Missouri. They passed cities made famous by Mark Twain, like his boyhood home of Hannibal on the Mississippi. It was a trip in the unknown, yet he loved the freedom of being on his own.

Like the itinerant traveler, with each mile taking him farther and farther from his home, his whole body loosened up and he took a deep breath as the train left Wichita Station, where he had the opportunity to get off the train and see the city's impressive station. He liked what he saw from the vendors selling candy, newspapers, gum, soda pop, to the shoe shine boy who, seeing him with the other colored recruits, gave him a big smile.

"You boys headed north up to Camp Funston, ain't you?"

The young shoeshine boy must have seen troop trains coming through on a regular basis and got to know the places they were headed. The young bootblack was no more than ten years old but exuded confidence and returned to spit-shine a vested suited customer reading the *Wichita Eagle*. No doubt, this young child was a hard worker. He had the calluses in his small hands to show for it. The strong odor of the black polish permeated the air, even overpowering the popcorn machine in the adjacent area. Looking around at the station crowded with soon-to-be inductees, his roaming eyes couldn't help noticing the stark separation of black and white troops. While many of the troops, both black and white, would nod to him, reality set in with the distinct bathrooms marked "colored" and "white." The vendors were accommodating and helpful, no doubt with a pecuniary aim in mind. Despite the moment, he knew once he arrived at the camp for basic, it would be a regimented and segregated environment headed by white officials. He just hoped that the commandants were nonjudgmental and intent upon making them soldiers. He smiled at the prospect of having his own bed too! *Even if it's a cot, it's mine and mine alone and I don't have to share.*

He thought of his brother and parents for a second before one of the Hinds County recruits, Jesse Jones, came up and said, "Our time is up; got to board the train."

James walked back to the train platform just as the time of the announcement of his train's departure. He purchased a bottle of Coca-Cola and went outside to board his train, catching up a few other colored troops in the cool late October weather. But he was in Kansas and ready for any eventuality.

These sites—cities, farmland of wheat, corn, and oats—were new and exciting. And for James, it was a continuing saga that he was about to embark on. His confidence, never in doubt, was reinforced by his physical presence that earned him the respect from his fellow recruits. As always, he got noticed by the other recruits, vendors in the station, train personnel, and curious onlookers who knew schedule of the troop train and wanted to give them a good send-off. He liked the attention but remembered what his mom had said as she gave him his bagged lunch: "Don't ever forget who you are, where you're from, and don't get a big head!" His mother wanted him to take a memento—something that had remained in the family for many years. She gave him a linen handkerchief that had been handed down from his grandmother in slave days. Lula Mae was given the handkerchief when her grandmother died and had kept it wrapped in the family Bible. Since she had no daughter to give it to, she always said she would give it to James's wife when and if he married. But the moment was ripe. Deep down inside, she hoped her son would come home from the conflict alive and well. Yet, with this war with its ever-mounting casualties, she felt it imperative to give him something that had not only a history to it but also had endured devastating episodes.

She wanted her eldest son to have it and eventually hand it down someday to a wife or daughter. That was her wish. So it seemed appropriate to give her oldest this family memento going off to war. Despite the fact that it was a lace handkerchief, it would be a connection to her and her family. James understood and carefully placed it in his bag. He knew what it meant for both of them.

He got to his seat and reopened up the brown bag his mom had so carefully prepared for him. His mom! A real saint who had given a fresh patch of warm fried chicken, rolls, mashed potatoes, and okra. Most of it had been consumed by the time the train arrived in Kansas. Although he had already eaten most of the goodies, he felt reenergized and consumed the rest of the brown bag lunch with gusto. Looking at the train, some of the local people started waving at the troop train. It was a nice touch to the soon-to-be troops heading overseas. He waved back to no one in particular, smiling, and before long the train left Wichita on his way to the camp. It would be a short trip to Junction City, Kansas. From there, it was a short distance to Camp Funston. Funston was part of the big site of Fort Riley.

The train arrived at Junction City, and James and other black troops from all over the South and Midwest were soon transported to Camp Funston. For a young man of eighteen, it was an epiphany, a new beginning, a new start. Part drama, part reality, it was an adventure—James's first adventure into the unknown.

Funston was part of the large Fort Riley. Commanded by Gen. Leonard Wood, it was one of sixteen divisional cantonment training camps organized by the US Army in the country. Wood, a distinguished army official, had a history of involvement from the Spanish-American War to the protracted intervention in the Philippines. In the Philippines, he was commander of Department of the East and a strong force against the insurrectionists headed by Emilio Aguinaldo. During the long, protracted intervention, Wood saw lots of bloodshed and torture inflicted on Americans. "Water-boarding," which was initiated by the Chinese and adopted by Aguinaldo, was leveled against the Americans. The Americans, learning the art of war, soon adopted it, resulting in more Americans killed in the Philippines than the entire four-month Spanish-American War. The brutal experience in the Philippines turned Wood into a no-nonsense approach when it came to war. Wood also was an early advocate of early preparedness when the World War started in 1914.

At Funston, Wood set out to do his job. Funston would be a big challenge but one that he took control. Camp Funston's objective was to train troops before sending them off to combat. With fourteen hundred buildings on two thousand acres, it was an impressive sight for James Hayes and the other recruits. A city within a city, for a small country youth, it was the largest structures James had seen. In all, it would fit the bill as outlined by the federal government by training fifty thousand troops.

Funston also was used for other purposes. It also included a detention camp for conscientious objectors, many of whom were Mennonites who were drafted and sent to Funston. Mennonites, like their Amish cousins, didn't believe in war and therefore didn't fight. Based solely on their religion, they would be in violation of a basic tenet of their faith if they took up arms or acceded to the army's orders. Added to the mix was their long hair and unusual dress. Their halting English made them a source of ridicule. Many considered these native-born citizens foreigners. The fact that they spoke German made some of the less-tolerant commanders question their loyalty as Americans. With war waging against the Central Powers, their refusal to fight became a contentious issue. It was a civil rights issue long before it was in fashion.

The experience of these Mennonites resulted in one of the most repressive aspects of the military in the war. Mennonites, many of hard-working, independent farmers from Missouri and Pennsylvania, were indeed exploited for their faith and tortured as a result. And they never complained to any officials or got the press's attention. The detention camp became a place where some horrible atrocities occurred. Many of these religious pacifists were beaten, called unpatriotic, and dragged by their long hair. In one case, several were hanged upside down above water and nearly drowned when the rope attaching them was lowered! This detention center was used throughout the war not only for deserters but also for conscientious objectors, such as these unfortunate Mennonites. Both were unfortunately lumped together as one. The treatment of the Mennonites was one of the worst episodes of what happens when war interferes with civil liberties. The detention camp at Camp Funston was a place to avoid and not discussed. It was a torture chamber long before twenty-first-century Guantanamo was used by the United States for suspected terrorists.

The detention area was separate from the rest of the camp, as were the black soldiers. The black troops wouldn't have any contact with either the detention center or the white barracks. When he arrived, James Hayes was assigned to one of the black barracks. He entered and looked around. What he saw was a long line of two-tiered bunk beds on each side of a single aisle. It was 43 feet by 140 feet and two stories high. Each barrack had a mess hall, adjoining kitchen, supply room, offices for commanders, and of course, dormitories. The dormitories had 150 beds in each section. The bed consisted of a single mattress. Camp Funston adhered to the segregated army that was rife at the time. Yet for someone like James, a poor sharecropper from one of the poorest regions in the United States, it was indeed an awakening. The grounds had a large general store full of supplies that made Hurley's look like a mere mom-and-pop shop. It also had a large social center used for assemblies, dances, military events such as graduations and promotions, plus a school for children of enlistees and an infirmary for the sick. By 1917, it had added a theater where silent films could be shown. It was a community that indeed had all the amenities that a small town would provide.

James, like all other prospective soldiers, was assigned to a particular bunk. He was given the lower bunk. Looking around, he took a deep breath and thought, *This will be the first time I have a bed to myself.* The bunks were standard issue, really cots with a single pillow and gray blanket over white sheets. For James, it would be home for six weeks. His time at Funston would indeed be an opportunity for him to show both himself and others his talents. Those gifts of strength plus a gifted voice would change his life forever. For now, he was just another poor, black soldier-in-training. By the time his time at Funston was over, he would be recognized and respected.

CHAPTER 10

Within a few days, James Hayes blended into the routine of basic training. He, like all draftees, would be up by 0700 hours at the sound of reveille. Told to have their beds made, they would then stand at attention in front of their bunks and get inspected. Beds were bound tightly, with blanket just a few inches below the pillow. The lockers behind the bunks had to shut tight, with no standard military uniform khaki showing. Recruits had to be out of the shower by 0630 hours, ready for inspection or any surprises. Nothing was to be said unless spoken to.

What usually followed was a two-mile jog around the periphery of the camp. Since many of the draftees were not in the best of shape, this exercise became theater for the drill sergeant, a not-so-sympathetic German-American named Henry Ham from Milwaukee. Given much latitude to do what he wanted to shape up his command, Drill Sergeant Ham wanted to have his charges ready whenever the barrack commander, Frank Lawson, came in with him for inspection. With a tough, non-compromising, and in-your-face attitude, he was assigned to the black barracks with little contact with blacks prior to this assignment.

The morning jog was Ham's show and dreaded by some but not James Hayes. The jog became a stellar moment. He led most of the joggers and was able to supersede even the boastful, hardened draftees from the urban areas of St. Louis, Chicago, and Detroit, who made fun of his country talk and accent. Through it all, James just grinned and did what had to be done, never questioning authority. He soon got noticed by those in command.

James got the respect that he had previously maintained in the cotton fields of the Mississippi delta. After just six days, his personality got him noticed with the higher ups. Ham approached him and told him to lead the two-mile run and said he would see him in his office, which was at the end of the barracks.

The two-mile run was not welcomed by some of the draftees who had led sedentary lives, unlike the fit and robust Hayes. It was followed by ten minutes of pushups, jumping jacks, and toe touches. This exercise, repeated three consecutive times, could be challenging for anyone not in the best shape. James was aware that not everyone would find the run easy. He again thought of his asthmatic younger brother. His empathy toward the more obese recruits by encouraging them to finish the task got him noticed by Lawson and Ham. What would follow would be a seminal event in his life.

Ham's commander, Frank Lawson, was a no-nonsense career soldier who had experience in the Spanish-American War fighting in the Cuban jungles in 1898. At forty-seven and six foot four, he made for an impressive sight. With a distinct Yankee accent, he was an anomaly to the black charges, many of whom never met a Northern Catholic. He was a native of Lynn, Massachusetts, from a poor Irish family whose roots went back to County Mayo, immigrating to Boston at the height of Potato Famine in 1848.

Assigned to the black barrack that housed James Hayes, Lawson was tough yet fair, not totally beholden to the segregated regulations. He remembered his Irish roots and the tough times his family had endured. His parents told him of the virulent anti-Catholic sentiment in antebellum period in Boston in 1850s trying to find adequate employment. The history of religious bigotry they endured had been handed down to him. His grandmother always told him not to judge people by their status or color but by their character. He used this as his mantra, and despite some grumblings from not having a military education at West Point, he managed to make his mark. His rise in the military was augmented by his stand in the Cuban jungles in the brief Spanish-American War fighting with Theodore Roosevelt's Rough Riders. Despite the War Department issuing wool uniforms to fight in the jungles of Cuba, Lawson proved to be a fearless cavalry unit leader. He was not given much recognition, yet TR liked the scrappy Irishman who related well to the men. The hero of San Juan Hill, Theodore Roosevelt came home to New York and was elected governor in 1898 and vice president on the McKinley ticket in 1900. As fate would have it, Roosevelt became president on the assassination of William McKinley. He quickly took command and made sure Lawson was recognized. Lawson ended up at Fort Riley in 1908 and took command of Camp Funston's black barrack when the United States entered the World War in 1917. With his family on base, he was popular with the black draftees who liked the fact that, as one of the recruits remarked, "He doesn't talk down to us." Indeed, his outlook was to treat everyone fairly. So he had some bonding, albeit from a different perspective to the raw, often suspicious, and scared young black recruits.

Sympathetic yet beholden to the rules, Lawson brought about a modicum of civility to the unit, and his barracks became a model for others to emulate. The other barracks, both black and white, were always told to model their barracks like Lawson's. Lawson demanded and got respect from the colored draftees assigned to him. His sense of fair play was always a virtue, and he demanded that the blacks assigned to him get the same provisions as the white draftees. Lawson also got to know the men assigned to him within a week. He got the lowdown on the raw new draftees, and Ham's report and appraisals were important to him. And General Wood wanted to keep a tight unit in all his barracks. Wood knew he could depend upon Lawson to make the right choices.

Lawson indicated to Ham that he wanted a very good, in-shape, and likable yet disciplined draftee to lead not only in the two-mile run but also in the daily calisthenics that would follow. Ham's order to James to report to the office was the reason for the encounter. It was just six days after his initial exposure to camp life and basics.

James Hayes was told to report sharply to Commander Lawson's office at precisely 0930 hours. Getting a written notice, typed by Lawson's secretary, Phyllis Ward, meant that something was happening. He prayed that his parents and brother were all right. It was with a bit of apprehension that he approached the office. Holding the note upon entering, he was instructed by Miss Ward to have a seat. She gave him a faint smile and no hint as to what would transpire. She returned to her typing, and James waited what appeared to be a long time yet was a mere seven minutes.

At precisely 0930 hours, James Hayes entered the inner office of Commandant Lawson. He was greeted by Henry Ham standing to the left of Lawson, who was seated at his desk. When Lawson saw the young recruit, he rose from his seat, wiping his hand with a paper towel.

Lawson had just enough time to extend his hand to James when the zealous drill sergeant Ham began, "This here is James Hayes. He excels in running and calisthenics and is popular with the other fellows. I even heard him sing with some of the others." This was an awkward moment for Hayes, who kept his eyes fixed on Lawson, wondering why he was called into the office. Lawson, who had inspected the trainees the second day, looked over the young, rigid man standing at attention.

"At ease, Hayes." Lawson walked over to where Ham was standing to the right of James. "Drill Sergeant Ham tells me that you're in good shape and have performed your duties admirably. And the music you and the other two sing is good for morale."

"Thank you, sir. I try to follow orders and do what is good."

With that, Lawson gave a nod, adding, "We need a leader for the colored unit here in the barracks. Ham has suggested that I assign you to lead the soldiers-to-be in the run plus the calisthenics. Do you think you're up to the job?"

"Yes, sir, but I don't know too much about being a leader." Hayes looked straight ahead at Lawson. He at last knew he wasn't called in for a family emergency or a reprimand.

"That's for me and the drill sergeant to decide. We might have a surprise visit from General Wood himself, and I want my men to be at their best. Do you understand?"

"I do, I mean, yes sir."

Hayes's voice had a shrill quality to it. He tried not to show his nervousness. He knew enough not to question others' assessment of him and would gladly take on the responsibility that was offered to him. Despite the fact that it was the first week of November, he felt sweat around his brow. He didn't want to show his uncertainty and tried to relax by breathing slowly. Never had anyone given him such responsibility. Back home, he was just another sharecropper, albeit a good, solid, and reliable worker.

"I also expect you to report directly to the drill sergeant if you see any hanky-panky going on." Lawson looked at Hayes, whose frown made him wonder if he what he was talking about.

"Do you understand?" Lawson was a no-holds-barred man who demanded an answer if he had any doubts.

"No, sir, can't say that I do." Hayes was clearly uncomfortable. All of a sudden, it seemed that he would have to be the person to look for and be wary of. He didn't want to lose his bond with his friends in the barracks. *I'm supposed to be a snitch on my own men!*

Lawson, glancing at his drill sergeant Ham, nodded and added, "What I mean is that I want you to report any possible fights or disagreements or drinking of alcoholic beverages or foul language to your drill sergeant. I run a tight ship here and have to get some of these dirt bags need some proper training. You report to the drill sergeant or directly to me. Is that clear?" Lawson's directive resonated with James, who realized that of all the recruits, it was he who would have some clout.

"Oh yes, I gets it."

Lawson, smiled at his grammatical faux-pas and added, "They tell me you're popular with the men. That's good. I also know a thing or two about singing." Smiling at Hayes, he felt he needed to tone down the volume a bit with a little humor.

"Nothing really; we just sing some songs that we knew back home.

Some of them are hymns that kept us busy in the fields and made the day go quicker." Hayes didn't know where the conversation was going.

"It's something, young man. It shows me that you can lead. Your attitude comes from your parents and good upbringing—right?"

James was starting to feel more uncomfortable, and the drill sergeant, sensing his unease, quickly interjected, "Whatever it takes to get this group together and united is fine by me. If you want to start a musical group, why the hell not! All that jive backwater music don't mean nothing to me, but if it keeps things in check, so be it!"

James Hayes had a big grin, as did Lawson, knowing that he and Ham had won over this young draftee. He knew music would soothe any agitated soul, and he was glad that this particular group of raw recruits assigned seemed ready to do what was expected. He didn't care if it were religious hymns, jazz, or ragtime. He sized up Hayes and felt he had made the right choice. James felt it was time to make a few statements. He looked down at the floor and then stood up erect and was ready to say a few words.

"Thank you kindly, sir. Me and the bunkmate of Jesses Jones—can't remember his name—and a guy named Beau St. Clair from Louisiana have a trio already, and I think one other fellow who I also forgot his name, know jazz. He wants to join up." Hayes was now in his space and felt much better. "But sir, I ain't no angel either. I mean I like to have fun and get out and dance and meet—"

"It's not about that. We expect you to meet up and relax after some tough drilling by Ham." Lawson's smile at Ham was acknowledged by a quick nod of approval. "We want you to be the leader we see in you. And I don't think you'll let us down, will you?"

"No sir, I'll do my best, my best," he said, repeating himself as if to emphasize his new orders. James's looked at the picture of President Woodrow Wilson and General John "Black Jack" Pershing on the wall, a wall that otherwise was drab white and in need of a good paint job. Looking at the pictures was clearly a distraction to mask his nervousness.

"Perfect. Tomorrow I'll show up before inspection and tell the entire barracks that you're in charge of the mile run and calisthenics under the wise eye of your drill sergeant, Sergeant Ham. Sergeant Ham will go over the routine with you. Don't fail me, you hear?" Lawson had his head down at eye level with James, who got the message.

With that, James Hayes, in just six days, had made himself known to the people who mattered—his superiors. The high-ranking officials in the segregated army who had no black to command an entire black troop. James, leaving the office that he had entered for the first time, started to return to his bunk. He wanted to get to the latrine and wash up before anything else.

He returned to his bunk, ready to go to mess hall for lunch. On his way, Jesse Jones, a fellow draftee from the delta, and Michael Strong of Chicago caught up to him, having seen him exiting the office of the commander. Some of his fellow draftees looked up and wanted to know what was going down. What was this all about? Was he in trouble? Going to be dismissed?

"What up with you, Hayes?" Jesse had known James, who lived a few miles from him in the delta and had worked on a nearby tract of land with his family. Like Hayes, his family was poor sharecroppers. Unlike James's family, Jones had three brothers working the field, and his absence wouldn't be as ominous as James's. Seeing him emerge from the commander's office sparked an interest in Jones. He knew James to be a scrappy, strong, and in-your-face person whenever confronted. He wanted to get the information. James walked up to Jones and Duggers, who were anxious to find out what happened in the inner sanctum of the office.

"They asked me to lead in the runs and with the exercises. Guess they wants one of us to make sure we're together and doing it right."

Hayes saw that his explanation wasn't what Jesse and his bunkmate, Franklin Duggers, wanted to hear. Giving each other quick glances, it was Duggers who had to speak up. Shaking his frowned head, he wanted to know why Hayes was called to the office. Duggers feared the worst. As an enlistee, he wanted out of his abusive home with his alcoholic father and his older siblings who constantly fought. He had given Hayes the once-over.' His first impression of Hayes was of a loyal, awkward sort who needed an education in a few practical things. "He's too country and goody-goody. Don't smoke, never saw him drinking when we hit the canteen in town." Duggers had to find out what went on. He wondered if things like staying beyond the curfew or maybe having a bit of contraband, such as liquor in the bunk, would make a rat out of Hayes. He needed to probe Hayes.

Duggers, a Detroit native, spoke up, saying, "Tell me you're not gonna spy on us, hear me?" Nodding at Jones, he added, "If we play a card game, talk some shit, or scheme a few things from the mess hall, swap some bullshit stories, talk about some women in not-so-fashionable way, you ain't gonna be in our faces, are you, man?"

James knew he had to speak up right now. The last thing he wanted to be was to lose credibility. He knew what a reputation a snitch had. It would make him a marked man. He would have to constantly watch his back. Given his own history of repression, he suddenly was confronted with the responsibility of maintaining a clean environment. It was a first crisis for him; he had to prove himself to be worthy and loyal to his fellow draftees while maintaining a somewhat privileged position that he savored once the offer was given. That offer made him feel like he was someone. The powers of the military in just the three days had liked what they saw in young James Hayes. Taking responsibility, he would not let his buddies get the best of him. He had no choice to face the men he barely knew and assure them that his task was one not to be a confidant or spy to the top brass but an advocate to the men instead.

He gave each of them a hard look, especially the skeptic, Duggers. Like a fighter in the ring, he wouldn't blink. The silence was deafening! Finally, James spoke up. "I'm going to be fair but just don't mess, okay?"

Exchanging glances with the two, he knew he had to do better. He explained what the conversation in the office was about. He stressed the need to keep the barracks clean and not allowing issues to explode. He explained that he would lead them in the daily run and exercises and if necessary, report an incident to the superiors. He wasn't going to be a lackey, but he would do his job. Looking at the two young men, he extended his hand, and they reached out and shook his in return.

"No need to worry about me, but don't fuck up guys!"

With that he turned his back and headed out into the late autumn air, smiling, knowing that he the confidence that the brass had seen in him. He felt good—real good as he picked up a small stone and threw it several yards. For a moment, he forgot about his scheduled mess hall lunch. He had won over the brass. More important, he stood tall when confronted with two of the most suspicious recruits. He had made his case about keeping the bunk safe and clean and adhering to the laws.

Taking a deep breath, he looked about and saw a familiar figure from the delta, Jimmie Ray Owens. The white barracks were located on the other side of the camp, and it came as a surprise to see Owens.

Extending his hand with a wide grin, he came up to James, saying, "It's good to see a hommie! I'm glad that we're at the same camp."

Hayes felt good seeing his friend from the delta. They exchanged stories about their trip by train and within a few minutes, Hayes said, "I guess we'll see each other on the grounds."

Knowing that the white barracks were off-limits, the brass kept the color line intact with minimum contact. Different schedules for morning run, calisthenics and sporting events, socials—it was in effect a segregated climate. Yet, Hayes, like Owens, was glad to see a homeboy, and they parted, knowing they would catch up at some point. James felt for Jimmie, knowing how his life up to now was not easy. The fact that Owens was considered some backwater hick didn't help.

Given the racial climate in America in 1917, Jimmie knew he had to be careful with his friendship with blacks. He was, in the end, a poor, sharecropper himself whose family had run-ins with the law and a sad history from an abusive, alcoholic father. Looked down by other whites, his family worked alongside some of the blacks in the fields. They kept a distance, but they still were on the same land. But here, like his fellow Hinds County friend, it was different. This environment for him was at once a chance to strut his stuff and make something of his dismal life. In James, Jimmie Ray found a sympathetic friend. Aware of his situation, James would have liked to bond more with Jimmie Ray but knew otherwise. Right now, he was presented with his own challenge and had to deal with it.

He had made up his mind. He had one restless night before this encounter, hearing the snores and belches from the bunks adjacent to his. That didn't bother him. James Hayes was glad to have clean sheets on his own bed, something he didn't always have the luxury of back home. The snores, occasional belching, and flatulence of some of the guys didn't faze him.

When he finally fell asleep, he had one of those dreams. A good dream. Maybe a harbinger of what was to occur the next day when called into his role.

His special angel in white dress appeared to him, smiling. She said nothing, but her radiance and light and beautiful presence were a sign that all was well. He had such dreams back home and now here. He took it as a sign to get on with the job he would soon be assigned. The angel in white had reappeared in a dream. Pointing to her heart, the message was clear. "Go with your heart and follow your heart." Faceless and yet radiant from the light, she seemed to tell him all would be well. Yes, he knew he would be okay. The job of getting these ragtag country and city boys together would be a challenge for him. But he would be there to put the men in shape while warning those who might stray to be aware of the consequences. *A rat, a snitch—never!* He smiled when he thought of it. *Me, a snitch! No, not me.*

His special designation became a clarion call to him that would project him into the next phase of his young life. Up to any challenge, part of the delta never left him. Wary of the intent of others yet respectful and loyal, he embodied the traits that the army so desperately looked for in a leader. He felt euphoric—of all the men in the barracks he was chosen! And he was eager, so eager to get on with life. He didn't have to wait very long. A real test was on the way.

CHAPTER 11

Within the next few weeks, it became apparent that James Hayes's selection as a group leader would have consequences. For better or worse, he took the job seriously. James, ever mindful of his special designation, became a force of good for the men in the barracks. In him, they found a friend they could rely on. Gone was the concern that he would be a stooge for the powers-that-be. Instead, he applied his new role in a very positive light, pushing for rights of the poor men in the barracks. Many, like James, had not strayed far from home. But unlike the more cautious and often timid men, James knew he couldn't stand for injustices from recruits and brass alike.

Hayes's sense of fair play soon became apparent when the raw troops started their daily routines. Given the fact that black troops were assigned to separate barracks on the far end of the camp was one fact. Another was the gall of the military to distribute Civil War uniforms to some of the black recruits—a war that ended in 1865! Stored and faded, the blue uniform of the former Union troops was an insult to the patriotic black enlistees and draftees alike.

The uniforms were given out in 1917, a stark contrast to the new uniforms given to the white troops ready for deployment in France as part of the American Expeditionary Force (AEF) under Gen. Pershing. Even more disgusting was the fact that it was now late autumn and the Kansas wind was unrelenting on the plains. Some of the black troops had to eat outdoors as there weren't enough seats at the canteen assigned to them. When he witnessed this, Hayes stormed into Lawson's office, asking why the black draftees had to endure the elements while there was plenty of space in the other white barracks. Aware of the strict segregation that was part of the army, he knew his barrack mates would never be assigned to the white canteen and eat alongside the white draftees.

Many of the black troops were from the Deep South in states like Alabama, Mississippi, Florida, and Georgia and didn't take kindly to harsh, raw weather. Being forced to endure the elements on the onset of winter was a real injustice. The information given to Hayes came from his fellow Mississippian, Jimmie Ray Owens. The poor white kid from his area who became a confidant to Hayes, often giving him the lowdown on what was happening. Owens also told James that the white draftees were talking about rumors of race riots in some barracks in Texas and East St. Louis and he should ask Lawson what he knew. These issues needed to be addressed, and James Hayes, taking on his new role seriously, felt he needed answers.

When asked about the injustices and the rumors, Lawson said he sympathized with the troops, but there were certain rules he too had to adhere to. He placated James by devising a rotating system whereby troops ate at staggered hours, thus avoiding having to eat outside on picnic benches adjacent to the black barrack. It was early November, and the temperature was nearing the freezing point. It was a moment of triumph for James, giving him respect and recognition from his fellow recruits. They knew he was no snitch but a solid leader who looked out for them. He also got Lawson to make sure the mail to family and loved ones got out in the same manner as the white troops'. His reputation grew, and with it, he got respect, knowing that the troops in his barracks had someone who would not back down. It also enhanced Lawson's reputation as a man who at least took his tasks seriously and tried to do the right thing.

James, given the assignment of group leader, took his job not only to shape up the troops but also to be the leader and advocate and voice for many of the poor, uneducated raw black troops. He multi-tasked well, going into Lawson's office to complain whenever a problem arose. As a result, there were fewer fights among the black troops than in the white barracks, and in one surprise inspection, the barrack was given a commendation from Gen. Wood himself. Yet, not all was perfect.

In one particular episode, he was nearly put into the brig when he stopped a fight between a white racist draftee who had used vulgar language against the black troops. When confronted, the white draftee, drunk from a night of carousing in the nearby town of Manhattan, backed down when Hayes, surrounded by several of the black troops, was able to diffuse the situation. Hayes took the man aside and despite his condition, had a few of his white barrack buddies take him directly back to his bunk. He had proven his worth, and his physical presence yet calm demeanor seemed to be the right mix. Soon, people took notice, from his buddies in the barracks to the kitchen staff and then, the higher ups. The word was out that James Hayes was a man of trust and honor. Within a few days, it was time for him to report to Lawson's office.

Called into Lawson's office, he stood his ground. Looking Lawson straight in the eye, he said, "Look sir, no disrespect, but you once said your family faced a lot of troubles. I understand that. I hope you know this—I won't let any of the men get beat up by some drunken asshole! It ain't right, sir, and I think you know that." Such a candid outburst was normally not tolerated by superiors, but Lawson knew Hayes was the real deal. He looked up at him, and moving his hand in a friendly wave gesture, he asked him to explain.

Hayes, sensing his moment, added, "I don't care what color he is—sorry, sir for that language." Lawson, who was sitting at his desk, never had such an encounter with any soldier—black or white. Getting up and walking over to Hayes, he extended his hand in friendship and said, "I know and appreciate that, soldier. I really do. But please know that I have to keep a tight crew here. Let's try to keep our barracks and our men away from this—"

"Sir, sorry to break in, but I won't let someone be put down not when he's right ..." Hayes, knowing that Lawson was a man of his word, would not back down. He had to get this off his chest. Lawson felt it was time for him to set the record straight, man to man, without any other personnel present.

"There is another thing, sir." Hayes was looking around at the blanched walls in need of a good paint job. He glanced at the windows, soiled from the recent rainstorms.

"Is this about the incident at the Wareham Theater?" Obviously, Lawson knew of an incident that left a lot of black troops uneasy.

"Yes, sir, it is." Hayes wanted to make sure the facts were right.

"Tell me, Private Hayes, what you know of this situation." Lawson had the information from the superiors and was interested in gathering facts from his trusted private. An order had been issued by from General Ballou labeled Bulletin 35. It had been issued and was to be read to the colored barrack later that day. Lawson was eager to gather whatever discussion he wasn't privy to with the colored unit. He depended upon Hayes to give him the facts as he knew them.

The issuance of the bulletin arose because of the management at the Wareham Theater. The manager indirectly had ordered that Negro officers and soldiers "refrain from exercising their prerogatives as citizens in the matter of attending public amusements or recreation, if their presence seemed offensive to the white patrons of such resorts and likely to provoke racial friction." Ambiguous and angering the colored troops in its rambling message, many asked what recourse they had. Was the theater in nearby Manhattan off limits due to the temerity of the local manager, afraid of angering a few racist patrons? Hayes needed an answer and would not back down. Waiting for an answer, he hummed one of his hymns to relax him, knowing fully well he might be in for a reprimand for being so candid. But Lawson, impressed by the cocky, young upstart knew he was the real deal. It was no secret about the event that had occurred at the local theater. It generated a lot of talk and got the newspapers' attention both locally and nationally.

The colored press was especially interested. James knew he had to live up to his fellow barrack buddies. Confused, the black recruits were desperate for an answer.

The town of Manhattan, Kansas, was 90 percent white, and the manager of the theater was catering to his public. He wouldn't have it any other way. And he wanted no trouble from the troops or his townspeople. He felt he had to react when patrons protested the presence of black troops in the theater. The theater manager wanted action and had approached the base commander when the black patrons refused to leave the theater.

Ballou, wanting to avoid racial strife that resulted in riots in bases at Houston and East St. Louis, walked a tight line. Actually, Ballou wanted the theater manager prosecuted for discrimination by the local district attorney. He felt that such action would appease the colored troops and avoid any further confrontation. His infamous Bulletin 35 was, he felt, a way to avoid conflict. Yet, it only added fuel to the simmering racial strife in close quarters in a small Kansas town. Its tone was patronizing, and the black press in the country, upon examining the order, had to react.

Ballou was angry that the full picture was misrepresented when the black newspapers, like the *Cleveland Advocate*, demanded action. The newspaper felt it was an insult to all black troops at Camp Funston. In an editorial, *the Advocate*, stated, "We expect better of Major General Ballou. The divide was made by white men—they can break it if they really care." Many newspapers, in fact, aware of the order wrote editorials denouncing it as an insult to the Negro race.

In the end, the manager was prosecuted and given a ten-dollar fine. But it still didn't sit well with many of the colored troops. Aware of this action, Hayes had given Lawson an earful to ponder. Many of his fellow barrack buddies said they had a right to attend a movie. They were drafted, and they were Americans. They wanted the support of the top brass, and Hayes was getting a mouthful from his friends. He demanded to see Ballou but was told he couldn't. James Hayes, the proud and loyal recruit, took his position as an advocate seriously. Coming into the office to see Lawson, he knew that his presence would alleviate some of the tensions. He wanted something from Lawson—his help and support. He mentioned that many of the men felt betrayed. Most of the black recruits lived all their lives in the shadow of Jim Crow. They had to live in a segregated society, aware of the repercussions that would happen if they violated or even questioned the status quo. They were indeed living in segregated Jim Crow but they sat in the reserved section in the theater balconies back home. The fact that they could attend the theaters in the Deep South was the issue here. At least they could attend. But it was not the case in Kansas.

Here, it was total rejection of patronizing a public place with no "separate but equal" accommodation that the infamous *Plessy v. Ferguson* decision of 1896 had required. That dreadful decision had legitimatized Jim Crow in the South. Segregationist and racist, this decision had an impact not seen since its 1857 antebellum *Dred Scott v. Sanford*, which catapulted the nation into Civil War. A near century of "separate but equal" made it possible for the South to inflict the injustices of segregation on the people of the South. People like James Hayes knew and were raised in such a climate. They knew where they were welcomed and what places to avoid. When it came to Kansas, it was apparent that a decision had to be made insofar as the interaction of troops with white townspeople. So Hayes wanted to know what would be done. He went over to confront Lawson.

Lawson was ready to reply to his young draftee. Yet, he was aware of orders handed down.

"I was right in selecting you. If fate would have it and this army was not separated by color, I would recommend you for a promotion. You deserve it. You should be doing my job, damn it! All I ask, for all of us and for our own safety, is that we watch ourselves and you watch your men and let's get through basics. Okay?"

Lawson returned to his desk, knowing that he had reach accord with Hayes. Looking at Hayes, he saw that he had touched a nerve. He could have reported him for insubordination by confronting him over the incident. He got himself involved because he knew he had to right a wrong. Not waiting for the KPs or any other officials, he took it upon himself and averted a disaster. Lawson was well aware of it and in his report, would highly commend him based upon the facts from both black and white recruits.

Hayes was assured by Lawson that since the incident didn't resort to violence and occurred off-base, he would like to ignore it. Yet the fact remained that he was the property of the US Army, and anything both in and off base was for him to act upon. Recent history wasn't kind in other parts of the country as it played out in Kansas.

Lawson knew tensions in the army were high. Lawson had gotten reports of black and white troops fighting at basic in Texas, resulting in a race riot. He wanted to avoid this cauldron from getting beyond his reach. With Hayes in tow, he felt the men—at least the black soldiers-in-training—would have a good, respectful, and fair representative in both Lawson and Hayes. The men of Lawson's barracks knew this too.

Over the next two weeks, Hayes performed his tasks better than expected. His fine physical shape made him at once noticed by other staff and soldiers. His marksmanship was most impressive; out of the 151 men in the barracks, he came out seventh and hit the target many times. When asked about his eagle-eye accuracy, Hayes, ever the modest one, shrugged it off.

"It ain't nothing. Always out in the woods around the Crawley land shooting possum, rabbit, and squirrel. Some birds too."

Hayes combined the humbleness of a person who knew life was unfair and just wanted to do what he felt was right. If anyone needed help, he remembered the values he learned from his parents: "Treat everybody the way you want to be treated." It was something he lived up to and was always aware, be it in the delta or at Camp Funston. Lawson as well as the at times retractable Drill Sergeant Ham knew he was someone in other circumstances would excel.

Called into Lawson's office one day after two-mile run and follow-up calisthenics, Hayes was told by Commander Lawson that an all-black division known as the Ninety-Third Colored Troops would be created. Ham and Lawson wanted to give an advance to Hayes, whom they knew would convey the information to the men. Just the night before, Jimmie Ray Owens and James had spoken about the training, which was coming to an end.

Jimmie Ray knew his unit would be headed to France and asked his commander in the white barracks, "What about the coloreds?"

His commander was a tough Kentuckian segregationist named Tom Fuller who, upon being asked, angrily shouted back at Owens, "Why do care about a bunch of ne'er-do-well soldiers? What are you anyway? They're never gonna see combat if I can help it."

Owens adroitly inquired if any unit would be formed just in case they were needed. Again, Fuller, an obese fifty-year-old something, brushed aside his hand and remarked, "Some of the higher-ups want to form a division. I guess you will tell your friends at the colored barracks, won't you?"

Owens, feeling uncomfortable at this exchange, indicated that he would not do any such things, as that would be Commander Lawson's domain. Fuller intensely disliked Owens; he had seen him in the company of James Hayes and other colored troops on the base and didn't like the fraternization. And he disliked Lawson, thinking him of as a Yankee do-gooder intent on integrating the troops. So Jimmie Ray casually dropped a hint the night before as he and Hayes discussed their possible deployment.

It was now eleventh hour. Most of the draftees had performed well. Except for the occasional out-of-shape recruits, most got through basics. A few were found not performing up to standards. Others had failed marksmanship; still others were too near-sighted, and a few more contracted venereal disease by getting drunk and hanging out in the town with loose women. Some were sent to the infirmary after a bout of influenza, which would be a worldwide epidemic by 1918.

By the time of Thanksgiving 1917, the Ninety-Third Division was coming into being. Aware that they would be given orders to deploy overseas, the camp held a big gala Thanksgiving in both the white and black barracks. At the dinner, General Wood showed up, along with Major General Ballou to assure the troops of their support. With the uproar over Order 35 still fresh in the minds of the black recruits, many felt slighted by Maj. Gen. Ballou's presence. Ballou's attempt to ease the tension did make a difference. Walking to each long table, Ballou stopped occasionally, talking to a few. Ballou sat with Lawson and make use of the great food in front of him.

Over turkey, cranberries, sweet potatoes, and pecan and pumpkin pies, a great dinner was held. A few volunteers from the local communities, such as the ladies of the Manhattan Methodist Church, brought both white and black troops some homemade goodies. Many of the ladies knew of the incident at the theater and had approached Gen. Wood in the hope of showing the good people of Manhattan. It proved to be just the right mix.

The troops, many away from home for the first time at Thanksgiving, liked the presence of the lady volunteers, many of whom made a special effort to bond with the boys. The fact that they came first to the black barracks meant a lot to the men. They were a presence that the men needed. This was true in both the white and black barracks.

The familiar smells of the homemade pies defused whatever lingering anger existed as a result of the theater incident. The ladies, told of the *a cappela* singing group led by Hayes, were serenaded by James Hayes and the other two members of his group, Beau St. Clair and Franklin Duggers. Given the occasion, the trio of singers, led by James sang, "Precious Lord," "There is a Balm in Gilead" followed by singing of the "Lord's Prayer." They also delighted both the troops and volunteers with a quick, lap-slapping version of Scott Joplin's ragtime music. James and his home-grown group of singers represented the strong, creative musical culture that came out of the delta. The popular music of the day—ragtime—had caught on with both black and white audiences. The working class delighted in ragtime, which originated in the brothels and saloons in New Orleans, Nashville, and the delta. It was a rich combination of sacred and secular sounds which told of the hardships of black lives. James was able to reach his fellow men in the barracks. The wild and complex rhythms of ragtime were addictive. It was a style freer and more natural, which cut into the social taboos of the day—love and sex openly expressed. Today James Hayes would reach the college students and nice church ladies as well using the syncopated rhythms and complex harmonies to create a distinctive style. They loved it! He knew his motley trio had talent, to everyone's delight.

One of the volunteers, Mrs. Anna Grayson, remarked, "That handsome lead singer is someone who has the talent to go somewhere." Mrs. Grayson, a member of her choir and the lead soloist, knew musical talent when she heard it. "Someday, we may hear more from that young man, mark my words," she added as the other ladies nodded in agreement.

The lady volunteers had heard of the incident at the theater and several spoke up, saying that the actions of the manager did not convey the sentiment of the town. The singing was well-received, and James ended it by singing a solo he heard on the phonograph. It was a new jazz song. This, plus the singing of a few hymns, did much to make the event all the more memorable.

As the dinner was winding down, the rumors about heading to the front in France were the topic of discussion. Many knew that it was just a matter of time before they were to head to the East Coast, board a troop ship, and enter the French ports of Brest or Le Havre. It was just a matter of time.

What happened next at Camp Funston would also be a life-changing event for James Hayes. General Wood wanted to organize a unit of black troops for possible transport to France.

CHAPTER 12

In early December, the Ninety-Third Division of Colored Troops got their orders to deploy overseas to the Western Front in France. For many of the mostly Southern young men, it would be their first time east. Told to have their belongings packed and placed in front of their bunks by December 11, they would head to Chicago by train and onto to Hoboken, New Jersey, right across the Hudson River from New York City. In Hoboken, they would board the *Leviathan*. The *Leviathan*, a former German cruise ship that witnessed many trans-Atlantic crossings, was confiscated in New York harbor once the United States declared war on Germany on April 6, 1917. It was the largest German ship on the seas and the pride of Germany, competing with the British and French liners. Its German name was the *Vaterland*. It was a 54,000-tonner and 950 feet in length. Her history from 1911 to 1914 witnessed many passenger crossings as a passenger ship on Hamburg American Line.

Once the United States entered the World War on the side of the Allies, the famous passenger ship and pride of the Hamburg American Line was seized by the US government. We were now at war with Germany, and its most famous passenger ship, which could travel up to thirty knots an hour, was a hot commodity. It seizure meant that the United States would soon use it as a transport ship. It was indeed ready to send our young, fresh troops to the trenches of France and give a much-needed boost to the Allies of Britain, France, Italy, and Russia.

It soon became a US Navy ship, ready for troop transport. All the young draftees and enlistees would soon be on their way across the Atlantic to fight the powerful German offensive. But the great ship still had a German name and insignia to change. Appropriately, on September 6, 1917, it was renamed and christened the *Leviathan* by President Wilson. It was a in-your-face moment meant to convey to the German Kaiser that the United States had not only seized their prized ship but also was ready to send its finest into battle. In early 1918, it sailed to Liverpool, England, and was repainted in the "dazzie camouflage" pattern in an effort to avoid the infamous and dreaded German U-boats.

Back in the United States in early 1918, the ship was outfitted to accommodate as many as fourteen thousand Yanks over to France. It would, over the next year and half, make many trips carrying even the future Hollywood actor Humphrey Bogart as a doughboy off to fight in France. And it would also transport the newly formed Ninety-Third Division out of Camp Funston, Fort Riley, Kansas.

The Ninety-Third Division was given their orders to move out and board the train to Chicago and then transfer at Union Station to another train to take them to New York. The order came right after reveille on January 6, 1918. A cold wind with some flurries made for a surreal setting. Interestingly, the night before, despite the snoring and occasional noise in the barracks, James was certain he heard the hoot owl—that same, familiar sound he was so used to in the delta. He briefly was awakened, but the constant albeit soft hoots made for a very comfortable sleep. This and his mystery lady in white dress served as an omen to him that all would be well. With the assurance of a person in control, he felt secure and safe even if it meant traveling in unchartered waters to a strange and foreign land.

The excitement in the air was addictive. Everywhere in the barracks, men made sure the pictures of their girlfriends, parents, pets, and friends were taken down from their small adjacent wooden drawers aligning each of the bunks. All their personal possessions—clothes, army gear, hygiene products, books, and any other mementos—were carefully put into their green canvas bags with their names and unit on it. The talk in the barracks over the Christmas holiday and the New Year's Eve party were preempted with the chatter. They knew they and the others in the camp would soon be leaving. It had been the first time most of the men were away from their families. For those enlistees who wanted to serve, and in many instances were fleeing abusive parents or the pain of segregation, it was not an unpleasant holiday. For James Hayes, however, it was different. Christmas was devoid of his mom's homemade specialties, especially the potato pie and the ham served with all the trimmings. He missed singing at Zion Baptist—the carols so familiar to him growing up made the holiday so special. Yet, here in the barracks, he was able to get his buddies to sing a medley of carols, including his mom's favorite, "Silent Night."

Christmas at Camp Funston gave the soldiers a chance to bond with each other before heading off. A committee was formed that included some of the local townspeople that were highlighted by a gala dinner replete with Christmas ham and turkey plus the traditional cookies. James thought of his dear mom and wished he was home to be with them. He wondered if Charles Atwood's wife gave birth. A smile came over his face as he thought of the two seventeen-year-old twin girls that would occasionally come by and say hello. Tipping his hat, they always had a nervous giggle for them. He hoped they were well, and also Mrs. Jane Hurley, who always treated everyone the same.

A few of his fellow bunkmates were down and depressed, not able to get home. The camp staff did their best to uplift their spirits. They had been through a rough, highly disciplined, and focused training. It was a test of wills and endurance coupled with the desire to achieve success. They were up early in the cold, running, and completing thirty minutes of exercises followed by daily regimen of detailed duty. Theses duties ranged from working in the mess hall, cleaning the barracks, attending seminars on what to expect once arriving in France, and learning to express oneself.

James helped to decorate the tree that was cut down in the nearby woods. It stood about sixteen feet high, and some of the more innovative men put makeshift ornaments made of paper, stringed popcorn, and tinsel. It helped ease the pain of being away from home. For most, it was a token albeit sincere effort to celebrate the season. In both the white and black barracks, the staff, directed by Gen. Wood, wanted the soldiers to feel appreciated. These actions helped.

A few of the townspeople brought homemade pastries and cookies traditional to the season. A grab bag was given to each of the soldiers from volunteers, and a surprise visit by "Santa'" made the day complete. It had a few necessities that the women from the Council of Churches had put together—socks, handkerchief, pens, writing pad, and some toothpaste. Several volunteer students from Kansas State University also were there to help. Many of the students bonded with the soldiers, given the fact that they were of the same age group. A few of them exchanged their addresses and asked them to consider writing while oversea. James was grateful; he still prized his heirloom handkerchief that his mom wanted him to keep in his pocket. He kept it in his right pocket at all times, carefully folding it. It would be a keepsake and a good luck charm. It was a reminder of his past that kept him attached to his home. Up to now, he had written three letters to his mom, knowing that Miss Jane at the general store would read them for him. He received one Christmas greeting from his parents. He knew from the handwriting that Jane Hurley wrote it for his mom. Included in it was a plea to be safe, knowing that "your mom and dad are always with you." James, grateful to get this correspondence before sailing out, would add it to his prized possessions.

Religious services, such as a Catholic Mass from St. Patrick's Church and a Protestant service held by pastor of First United Methodist Church, were also held separately at the barracks. The white barracks also got the same from the women of Manhattan, Kansas. The officials knew that morale was an issue, given the circumstances at the Wareham Theater. The presence of both the college undergraduates and the church ladies was a big boost. The commanders knew they had to act as quickly as possible whenever a sensitive subject, such as race, entered into the discussion. The fact that Camp Funston was able to avoid the violence and vitriol that was rampant at Houston and East St. Louis was a credit to both the individual soldier and the commanders. Many attributed the diffusion of tension the active result of James's intervention to avoid a fight.

Admired by both the top brass and the average doughboy alike, James was asked to say a few words at the Christmas event. He got up and looked around, and smiling and nodding to the troops and feeling very confident, he proudly announced, "Us colored men are fighting for the same thing as the white man. We both deserve the same respect. Our blood spills the same color as the white man." Following this brief tribute, there was sustained applause.

Both Lawson and Ham, knowing that they made the right selection in choosing Hayes, exchanged glances that spoke volumes. It was in large part to James Hayes that a serious incident was avoided. They knew it and so did all the troops, both white and black. A bit of a celebrity status for the quiet James Hayes. It took a country boy, not quite nineteen, with little schooling and a lot of heart and decency, to avert a major crisis. That he was talented, with a gifted voice and an unassuming demeanor, made him all the more likable.

The Ninety-Third Division, ready to leave for the front, knew that they would still be subjected to ridicule, discrimination, hatred, and second-class citizenship. They were far from being "separate but equal" that the infamous *Plessy* decision declared in 1896. In the two decades following the high court ruling, the South had become a Jim Crow environment. It deprived the black man the right to vote through a series of Jim Crow Laws. What emerged as the troops, both black and white, going off to war in early 1918 was a country divided. With Mr. Wilson as chief executive, it saw no further advance in civil rights. Brought up in the South, the president, a believer in segregation, actually expanded the separation at the federal level in Washington. The black troops knew they would be fighting for America and were proud to do their duty. Yet, the fact remained that these able troops would be relegated to menial tasks due to the pigmentation of their skin. America in 1918 had a long way to go in the area of civil rights. These troops knew, if ever given the chance, they would have to prove themselves to be above criticism and ridicule by excelling at all the jobs thrown at them.

But, there was something else. And it was important. They also knew they could fight, shoot, march, and organize as well as any white division. Yet, they also expected the inevitable—that their talents would be again relegated to common chores, such as unloading and loading supply ships, cleaning latrines and mess halls, working in triage areas after battles, and burying the dead. They could do better, and many wanted to show the segregated US Army that they had what it takes to get on with it. It would take the horrors of the battle scene to change things. But things would indeed change. Right now, they had to pack up, travel by train to the East Coast, and set sail on a reconverted, captured German passenger ship converted into a transport troop ship. James Hayes was ready for any eventuality that awaited him, and he was one of the first to board the *Leviathan* on a cold February morning in Hoboken, New Jersey.

CHAPTER 13

The train trip across the Midwest from the heartland of America to the East Coast was for James Hayes a transformative one. It was his first trip on a train headed north. Stopping briefly in Chicago, he got a glimpse of the beautiful Union Station, replete with the columns and marble that made it a replica of a long-gone Roman temple. He marveled at the architecture and the tall buildings coming up along Lake Michigan as the train left the station and headed into the Indiana countryside. Traveling through Ohio, he saw how the farms of the north differed from the ones back home in the delta. *These farms got more wheat, oats, corn. It's so unlike back home where we worked on cotton fields.* His fellow travelers in the segregated car were almost all from the Deep Southern states of Louisiana, Alabama, Georgia, Arkansas, and Mississippi. Many, like young James, saw the factories and small mills when the train went through parts of Pennsylvania. They also saw the big steel mills at Homestead, outside Pittsburgh. It was quite a sight for these first-time travelers on their way to the East Coast. James thought of his family as the train inched it way. He knew that the white troops were up in the next two cars. He thought of his friend, Jimmie Ray. He knew he was in one of the three cars up.

The overnight trip to Hoboken was met by a brilliant albeit cold winter sun. James, bleary-eyed from a fitful sleep in an upright chair, squinted at the sun as the train came into the Hoboken station. Adrenalin flowing, he and the others on the right side of the train had a panoramic view of the great city on the horizon. Scrambling over to get a better view, they stumbled over each other, shouting and cheering as the skyline grew closer.

That skyline of New York City, directly across the Hudson, provided a lot of chatter in the car as the men stared at the largest skyscraper in Lower Manhattan, the Woolworth Building. Completed in 1913, it was called the "Cathedral of Commerce" and could be seen clearly twenty-five miles away. The young, vulnerable, and naïve men, many still in their teens, could only dream of seeing the city from the top of the building. The lure of the big city would have to be put on hold for now. It was not to be. They were troops, and they had to quickly disembark the train and board the giant troop transport ship that would take them across the Atlantic. The big city, its lights flickering in the early morning light, would have to be put on hold for now.

Like the big city across the Hudson, the giant ship, docked at the end of the massive pier, was a sight to behold. As tall as a ten-story building, its camouflage colors of green and white were painted in the peculiar pattern. Its colors were to thwart the infamous and deadly German U-boat submarines that were menacing the North Atlantic. With deadly results, the German submarines had inflicted much damage and loss of life competing with the might of the world's largest navy—the British Navy.

The situation on the ground was not much better. Bogged down in the wet, cold trenches in Northern France, the war, by early 1918, was reaching a crucial stage. As James and his fellow soldiers boarded the *Leviathan*, the war was at a stalemate. The fresh Americans could hopefully turn the tide. And they had quite a job to do!

Their job involved transporting their gear and getting themselves on the massive *Leviathan* docked in Hoboken. Like an enticing young coquette, it became the talk of the troops as they ascended the gangplank and boarded the transport troop ship. Inciting and foreboding, it was for many of the troops their first time aboard any ship. For James Hayes, it was a surreal moment.

The great New York skyline ever ascending upward in the early twentieth century plus the frenetic pace of loading the ship with supplies and men added to the excitement of the moment. James, and no doubt others, envisioned his trek as a rite of passage, leaving behind the scars of his time in the delta. The fact remained that they were expendable troops going to war. Many wouldn't be returning. But that was the last thing on young James Hayes's mind. This was an adventure, a job, and something he was prepared to do.

When they arrived at the gangplank, James and all the other troops that had been on the train were handed a slip of paper. This was known by its French name, "billet," meaning ticket. Both Ham and Lawson were on hand, having ridden in the segregated white car. They instructed the men not to lose their billet. The stoic captain, Michael Scanlon, scanning the black troops, shouted above the din of the noise of cargo being boarded, "This slip is proof that you belong on this ship. It also tells you where you live, sleep, eat when you are on board. Do not lose it!" *Even at this moment, he gots to tell us he's the boss.* James, shaking his head and grinning broadly, swung his bag over his shoulders and walked up the gangplank. He was ready for any eventuality.

Arriving at the top of the gangway, stepping on board the ship for the first time, James and the other colored troops were directed to the berthing space. They were told that the berthing place is where they would "live, eat, and sleep during the crossing." Several uniformed men showed James and the men from Camp Funston to their assigned berth.

Looking around the assigned quarters, he saw the cramped bunks. They were really cots consisting of strong canvas hemmed down on the sides. Supported by four iron uprights for the rough seas, three upright bunks allowed for maximum usage of space. Each bunk had a number corresponding to the billet number assigned to each soldier. James's number was 407. He was assigned the top bunk.

These quarters were the same for both the white and black troops. Each bunk had a life preserver, which had a number matching the billet number assigned to each man.

The bunks themselves, similar to the ones they had at Funston, were six feet long and three feet wide and were always cleaned and disinfected after each crossing. In such tight quarters, cleanliness was a priority. There were washrooms and showers, and each soldier was asked to do his part to keep all areas of the ship clean. This former passenger German flagship had been totally remodeled and made suitable for the fourteen thousand men traveling from seven to ten days to the port of Brest, France.

James Hayes and the other men assigned to his unit were told to go on deck after boarding for a greeting and orientation from the ship's crew. For Hayes and everyone else on their first voyage, the ship was like a home. Its kitchens or galleys and floor or decks would become familiar in the long crossing to Brest harbor. And like most former passenger ships, the reconstruction of the ship made for tight quarters. It was built of bulkheads and decks, with many passageways connecting the sleeping quarters or compartments. These compartments were lettered, such as A deck and B deck, according to the number of decks. James was assigned to C deck.

Michael Sawyer, the captain of the *Leviathan*, was a fifty-one-year-old career navy man. He had two previous crossings with the former German passenger ship. A native of Pittsburgh, he was a proud Irishman who family had emigrated during the famine from Limerick.

His job was to make the men feel comfortable, knowing the rough seas in the North Atlantic would be challenging to some, resulting in *mal de mer* or sea sickness due to the constant movement of the ship. He wanted the raw, naïve, and vulnerable men to be aware of what lay ahead.

His message this morning before embarking would be brief and to the point: "You will be part of the great movement of troops to Brest, France. Each of you will do your part. Let us hope for a calm and easy crossing. But I must tell you, you will experience a very peculiar sensation at first. Most of you have not been on the high seas. But you will get used to the sensation of the movement. Remember to keep your feet more separate when walking on deck. Throw your weight on one side, then the other." At this point, the captain instructed each soldier to try it out. He went on to explain, "That little reminder will help if and when we experience rough seas. You will have a good appetite from all this craziness. You will be provided with a hearty breakfast. I strongly recommend that you eat, no matter how you feel from the sea effects."

The captain instructed that no smoking was allowed at night. "The enemy can spot even a mere light from a distance. We want to avoid the opportunity for the enemy to engage us. Although we'll be outside the war zone in the Irish Sea, we have to be mindful that we are at war and have to take every precaution. The glow of a cigarette may be seen at a distance of one-half mile. We, therefore, could be a target, and we don't want that!" The captain went to say that if anyone was caught smoking he would be placed in the brig until the ship docks at Brest.

It was now apparent to everyone on board how serious this war was and that they would be an extension of it. James went back to his quarters, and he and his two singing buddies went up on deck as the ship was ready to disembark. They wanted to get a glimpse of the New York skyline as it sailed down the Hudson, past the Statue of Liberty, getting a glimpse of the Brooklyn, Manhattan, and Williamsburg Bridges.

The sites of the great city made him want to one day return. Turning to his friends, he proudly announced, "Once we're finished with this war thing, we're gonna get a gig at one of the clubs, complete with our group and some musical instruments."

He envisioned all the attention from the pretty ladies to the people who could contract his group to sing in the clubs with big bands that were becoming popular at that time. After that, he would be rich and famous and go back to his home just to visit and help his family. A dream. He reached into his pocket and took the lace handkerchief that his mom gave him. His connection to her, the folks back home, and the people he left behind. He thought of the lady in the white dress. *Maybe she be waiting for me when we gets to France.* Looking at the city as the ship made its way down the Hudson, he saw the famous lady in the harbor.

James, seeing the Statue of Liberty, started singing "America," which was joined by the majority of the black troops assigned to their deck. St. Clair and Duggers came alongside him, adding to the volume and inviting others to join. Their voices could be heard in the upper decks, resulting in the white troops joining in. In unity in song at least the black and white troops were united as one sailing off to a fate unknown. Despite their uncertainty and the knowledge that not all would be coming back, they were indeed united in spirit. The music had a mellow effect, causing the captain himself to remark, "I've been on three crossings. This is the first time I experienced this. I want to know who the young man on the colored deck is responsible for this spontaneous singing. He did more by getting the troops together to sing than I could in my message to them."

Once again, unwillingly and unknowingly, James Hayes had made an impact on the people around him from the nervous first-time troops to the superiors. A sense of pride coupled with his Southern modesty and good upbringing made him a figure that others gravitated toward. His standup to the commanders at Camp Funston was known and appreciated by his fellow black troops. They knew in him they had found someone who would not back down when an injustice needed to be corrected. It wouldn't take long for him to impact on the captain and others on the crossing. His presence would become known, and before long, he would be asked to perform in front of the troops.

CHAPTER 14

The crossings proved to be uneventful as far as dangerous U-boats sightings and the weather were concerned. Despite the midwinter cold, the sun shone bright on deck for four straight days, followed by light snow mixed with rain for the next consecutive ones. By the time the *Leviathan* docked in Brest, it had been a full eight days at sea.

For James Hayes, the crossing was not only a chance to get away but also a learning experience. It also was a wake-up call that allowed him to discover his talents. He started going to the library on the second day of the eight-day voyage.

Before leaving Funston, Lawson had given him an English grammar and speech book, adding, "You'll never go places without command of the language. This is my gift to you. Keep it and treasure it as you do that handkerchief of your mom's."

James knew his command of English grammar was poor and kept him at arm's length from others. He had only been to the equivalent of third grade in the small, overcrowded, segregated school back home. He wanted to speak properly and decided it was as good a time as any to achieve that goal. He stepped inside the ship's library, asking the attending seaman to give him an additional English grammar book. His entry into the small space was from someone who saw his potential.

James found himself in the library, studying grammar at the encouragement of his superior officer at Camp Funston, Lawson. He always remembered Lawson adding, "You need to polish up on the King's English, young man, if you want to make your mark."

James became a devoted student whenever his duties as mess hall staff didn't interfere. Even in the confines of the ship's kitchen, he went over and over the correct English grammar and speech patterns. It became his passion, and soon he and others noticed the difference. Words had power, and the proper usage had strength. He would self-educate and emerge, as he did in other endeavors, above the fray. Proud and with confidence, he was unafraid to speak up for his fellow ship mates, be they white or black.

It was in the mess hall kitchen that another momentous event occurred. It was the third day at sea. He encountered an Italian of first-generation parents from the upstate Saratoga County community of Mechanicville, Vincent Valenti. Valenti, although assigned to the white berth, quickly became friends when James started singing to pass the time in the mess hall kitchen. Like James, Vincent Valenti was assigned to prepare foods, such as salads, and put bread and glasses on the long rectangular tables that served as the dining areas for the troops. Valenti, drafted by the local board upstate, previously had a four-piece band that played at resorts such as Saratoga Springs and nearby Lake George in the summer and was invited to perform in Albany for the inauguration of the current governor, Charles Whitman.

"Word is out, Hayes, that you have a fine voice. That you were the man who started singing 'America' as we passed the old lady in the harbor."

Vincent saw a smile on James's face when mention of the spontaneous singing occurred two days earlier as they passed the Statue of Liberty. Valenti had heard his voice in the mess hall but wanted a reaction from James. Valenti, diminutive in stature at five foot six next to the tall, well-built Hayes, had a proposal.

James gave Valenti a good look over before adding, "Some people think so." Remembering what he learned the night before in his English grammar book, he added, "Some say so. My buddies from Funston, Beau and Franklin, sing good too—I mean well."

Valenti smiled and knew that it was time for him to explain where he was going with the conversation. He asked James if he and his two others, Beau and Franklin, wanted to form a group. Valenti had bonded with a Wisconsin clarinet player, Wes Morgan. Like Valenti, Morgan had performed at various functions, from weddings to parties, in his native Racine, Wisconsin. Valenti played piano and was told by Morgan that a saxophonist from Newark, Delaware, Tom Ricker, wanted in as well. Ricker, Valenti, and Morgan were all assigned to the white deck and had met to discuss the possibility of getting the music group together to pass the time and possibly perform before disembarking at Brest, still six days away. So, Valenti took the initiative. He decided to approach Hayes.

"We should ask the captain or someone in control of events if we can practice and maybe perform. You in, Hayes?" James gave his iconic infectious smile, and Valenti knew the answer.

It was now time for James to speak up. "I know some of the men won't mind us mixing and getting a group together, but there's still a lot of hate toward us."

Valenti, nodding and frowning, added, "Hey, I don't give a goddamn what they say. I've been called a dago and wop, and I don't give a shit about that. Sorry to be so blunt."

James smiled, knowing that Valenti was sincere and wanted to try to get a group together, although ignorant of these disparaging ethnic remarks directed at Valenti. But he liked his candor. He knew he could trust this man.

"Vince, is that your name, or shall I call you Vincent?" Hayes inquired.

"Vince, Vinny, doesn't matter." Valenti knew that Hayes was feeling him out and wanted to find out how sincere he was.

"Tell me, Vince, can you play ragtime?" Vince gave James a puzzled look. He knew where this was going. Being tested and making an introduction was one thing. He now had to step up and prove that he was serious.

"Just give me a chance and I can play anything on that piano. I heard Morgan on that horn, and he's good—real good. Let's give it a try. We need to talk to someone." Valenti was excited at the prospect. He knew he had gotten to James.

"Okay, let's go to the captain's office and asked him if we can make history!"

Valenti was all smiles and had to add, "We got to see if the others want in. I think they will. Will you have any problems with the other singers in your group?" Valenti knew that the issue of race was sensitive and wanted to give Hayes latitude and connect with St. Clair and Duggers.

"I have to ask them. I been spending a lot of time in the library these past two days and haven't spoken to them. They like to play cards and pass the time like that." Vinny had to speak up and reassure his new friend that they should give it a go.

"Maybe it seems a little stupid to form a group with only six days to go at sea. But let's see if we have something in common. I love ragtime. I know you do too. Scott Joplin's 'Easy Winner' is one of my favorites, as is 'Maple Leaf Rag.' You're familiar with these, right?" Valenti wanted to know the extent of Hayes's knowledge.

"Sure, I heard them both. I know St. Clair, who's from New Orleans, hums one of those tunes all the time. He's worked the clubs as a singer and dancer. Yeah, let's go and see someone now."

James knew he had to win over his other two friends, Beau and Franklin. Of the two, Franklin, from Detroit, would be the more difficult to win over. He, like James, had firsthand experience with hate mongers and wasn't afraid to speak up. James knew he had to muster enough strength to win him over. It didn't take long for the word to get out that James Hayes and Vince Valenti wanted to form an integrated group of musicians. Franklin Duggers left his card game and walked directly up to James Hayes with curled lip and frowning. The message was clear to James Hayes—Franklin Duggers needed to be won over. But first he would give his friend James an earful. Hayes wouldn't be disappointed but was determined to win over his recalcitrant friend.

"Hey, James, what's this bullshit?" Duggers had heard rumors and wanted answers from his friend. He walked up to him after eating. James was clearing one of the tables and seeing Franklin approaching, put down the tray of soiled glasses to take to the kitchen.

Franklin looked James directly in the eye and got back the same in-your-face look from the tough James Hayes. Similar to the encounter at Funston, Duggers was convinced that Hayes's motive was suspect and that there was a sinister edge to all this talk going in the black deck. Duggers's family had their roots in rural South Carolina before moving as part of the Great Migration to the North in 1912. Duggers, like James, knew the degradation of Jim Crow and never forgot the treatment his granddad endured when, as a child, he was forced to wait for medical attention that clearly caused his grandfather's death. Waiting two hours after what was a heart attack, the damage was done, and his grandfather, Mitchell Duggers, died with him there in the waiting area, unattended. His rage was evident now that Hayes wanted to inculcate a diverse group of musicians. Hayes set out to win over his friend.

"Okay. I was going to talk to you and Beau about an offer."

"Offer—what offer? To keep letting the staff use us more. No way, man!"

James knew he had to act and act quickly. He wiped his hands on the white apron and, taking off the apron got closer to him. "I'm not going to let your attitude, anger and frustration gets in the way." Hayes could see that Duggers was listening. "You think you're the only one who has been through this crap. You're not. I'm not going to say that your situation shouldn't be forgotten …"

"James, what the fuck are you trying to tell me?" Franklin wanted to know what he really had to say. "Cut to the chase, man, and stop the bullshit with me!"

"I need you to stay with Beau and me and sing with musicians—white musicians that want us to sing and form a group. I don't know if we'll even be able to form a group and practice, but I'm going to approach someone in authority." Hayes paused, letting Franklin absorb the moment.

Franklin had a big smile, adding, "You know, brother, you're reading that book and you sound like a white boy. Have you forgotten who you are!"

James had had enough and exploded, "My family is still in the delta. My mom works her ass off, as does my dad. My own uncle was killed by the Klan. Do I need a lecture from you—no! So, I'll you again—are you with me?" James looked hard at Franklin Duggers, assured that he had made an impact. He waited for him to respond. He stared him up and down.

"Okay, if that means anything, I see you really want this gig and maybe you'll do something good. But if these crackers mess up, I'm out, you hear?" James knew he had won over Franklin Duggers and felt that his first hurdle was accomplished. Smiling, he reached out to Duggers, gently touching him on the shoulder.

"Why don't you ask that captain to let us mix and fight too like the white troops!" Duggers couldn't resist the opportunity to express the frustration that most black troops, including Hayes, felt.

"Let's first work on this. The white guy I met is from New York State and really wants us to connect. I told him that I needed to talk to you and Beau. I knew you would be a hard sell, but you would give it a shot. I know you care, Franklin. So do I." James, ever the diplomat, wanted his friend to know that he valued his input.

"Man, that would be earth-shattering if old Wilson allowed us to fight." James extended his hand to Franklin and gave him a high five. James added, "I want you to come with me to meet the others in the group and see the captain—okay?"

"Okay—I don't want to be sorry I did this." Duggers still had some doubts.

"Well, sometimes you have to stand up and do something yourself. They like our voices, so let's put it to some good use. Who knows? Maybe, we'll perform in some fancy ass club in Paris!" Hayes was in a good mood and was ready to tell Valenti about his coup. He looked forward to meeting up and hearing what the other musicians—Morgan and Rikers—would have to say. For the moment, he had won over his tough friend and proceeded to go to the library for a thirty-minute study period on English grammar. "I sound like a white boy!" He laughed at the comment that Duggers had directed and knew it was an indirect compliment. "Good one, Duggers!" Duggers, not smiling, wanted to find out the real deal.

As for James, he would utilize the good grammar to his advantage but never forget his roots and his family. He reached in and took out his handkerchief, which he had just washed, and clutched it, thinking of what his family was up to in the delta. He thought of his brother and wished he could get the medical attention that was denied to Duggers's grandfather. He understood Duggers's reluctance to accept the offer given him. He appreciated his struggle and knew it was a bold step for him. Like the acceptance of Hayes as a leader and spokesperson at Camp Funston, it was good to have a person like Duggers around. He was a reminder of the pain and constant struggle that was ongoing in the Jim Crow South. Hayes was much more forgiving but was stronger in character and temperament and willing to try changes, even if those changes involved baby steps. He was ready to take up the mantle and get on with the next phase of his life. The fact that he had won over Duggers was a major accomplishment. He felt good about that. He navigated what could have been a disaster in the right direction, getting his vocal group together. But the job was not over.

It was now time to gather the group together and plead their case to the captain or someone in authority. He was ready for whatever decision awaited. He knew this wasn't going to be easy, given the strict segregation even aboard the *Leviathan*. There were separate quarters for whites and blacks, and the dining hall, now a mess hall with its elongated, plain rectangular tables, was also segregated. Mixing was done only in some areas common to both: the library, the infirmary, and the Sunday services, depending upon your beliefs. Yet, the men knew the situation, and few incidents occurred.

James Hayes had been through so much in his eighteen years on earth. He realized he had the chance to make a difference, and he would follow up with this bold proposal. *Music always brings people together.* He remembered those words from Pastor Atkins when he was just a boy. Now was the time for action. The worst that could happen was a rejection; yet he was ready to take that chance.

CHAPTER 15

James Hayes had no problem getting Beau St. Clair on board. St. Clair, a native of New Orleans, was used to an integrated crowd when he performed, despite the Jim Crow laws in the state of Louisiana. With Duggers now skeptically aboard, he got Valenti to bring the other musicians, Riker and Morgan, to meet with his trio. They immediately bonded. They performed after just a few practice sessions, once the officials on board saw the benefits.

As the impresario and lead vocalist, James had no problem getting his other two singers to learn the lyrics of the latest ragtime hits, "Russian Rag," "Maple Leaf Rag," and "Top Linen Rag." The fact that Tom Riker had copies of the lyrics and music made the music end of the ensemble able to connect. The matchup of vocals and musicians practiced for three straight days. There were still three days from Brest and decided that a performance could be held for two consecutive days on board the main deck of the *Leviathan*.

The captain, Michael Sawyer, a native of Washington State, was impressed with Hayes's presentation in the company of all the musicians and singers. They gave Sawyer a brief taste of what they could present. Sawyer, a lover of ragtime, had no problem in getting the project off the ground.

"You men can do so much good by giving back your talent on this crowded ship."

Sawyer was aware of the lack of entertainment—with fourteen

thousand men on board, there were no ample supply of women to meet. The few nurses in the infirmary were, for the most part, older and very busy, with little time to socialize. Sawyer liked the idea of an integrated group and felt it was a great idea to alleviate the tension as they approached dangerous waters nearing the French coast. Despite the cold, damp weather, it was decided that the deck could accommodate the large number of men who needed relief from their duties and the constant reminders of the pending trench warfare they were destined to be part of.

James was ready for the big event. He and Valenti would serve as hosts and ask for any requests. "Let's make sure the fellows enjoy the session. Some of us may not make it back, you know and I want to make it special."

Hayes liked Valenti, and he asked if he knew of any comedians or funny guys who might want to consider telling some jokes between their jams. Valenti knew a fellow from Fresno, California, who like to tell jokes. His name was Larry Suarez, a short, stocky guy with an uproarious laugh. According to Valenti, he liked to be the butt of his own jokes, an early version of a Rodney Dangerfield. It would be a good mix with the music. When asked by Valenti if he would relate some of his jokes, he jumped at the chance. So, it was all set. The program, put together hastily, would nevertheless hopefully be a big hit with the fellows aboard. They needed some levity to ease the boredom, drudgery, and tedious routines of being at sea for eight to nine days. The ship's captain, knowing that his controversial decision might not go well with all the troops, nevertheless gave his approval.

"My job is to get this tub into port on time and with minimum problems; if these young men want to express themselves through song and comedy, so be it!" With that settled, it was agreed that the entertainment would be on Saturday and Sunday at 2:00 p.m. on the main deck.

Word spread quickly, and the group soon became the subject of much discussion. Taking a cigarette break from his assigned duties of washing the deck, Beau St. Clair approached James Hayes. From the look on his face, he knew he was about to hear some news.

"James, you know we do sound good, don't we? I even like the idea of getting the music group together with those white boys. But ..."

"What's the problem, Beau? You getting some flak from some of the brothers?" James knew he had to be an advocate for change. He wanted to make sure that all was set for the upcoming gig slated for the next day.

Beau wanted to reassure James. "You know I'm with you one hundred percent. Some of the men want to know what you had to give up to ..."

"You know me better than that. I'm not going to give up anything when it comes to us."

James knew that there were suspicions that haunted him from Funston when he was tapped to be a role model and lead the men in exercise routine. Now with rumors flying about the upcoming event, men in the black bunks wanted to feel that their contributions via James and his vocal trio would be given proper and deserved recognition. More importantly, they wanted to make sure that they would be treated fairly and seated where they wanted.

The weather, always a factor on the high seas in the North Atlantic in February, became the catalyst for change of venue. Gusty winds coupled with constant, cold waves on main deck made the decision an easy one. The crashing sound of the waves and the constant winds wouldn't allow those in back area to hear anything. There had to be a better place.

Instead of freezing in the open air on deck, James suggested that the event take place in the beautiful Beaux-Arts theatre aboard the ship. It would make a great impression for all to see the integrated musical group perform. For some of the black troops, it would the first time they set into the main floor of a big theatre. Aware of the sensitive nature of race, he went to see the captain with Valenti.

James got the captain to move the venue to the former passenger ship's big theater with a grand stage. He made it clear to the captain that the men of color would not be relegated to the balconies but could sit wherever they wanted. He knew most of the black troops were from the Deep South and had to sit in separate sections. Those sections were usually in the balcony, where those with vision and hearing problems were always challenged. James wanted no part of this Jim Crow world on board. He and the other troops were already separated in their sleeping quarters, occupying the lower decks, which felt the impact of the bad movements on the high seas. Since they had an integrated group of singers and musicians, he and Valenti agreed, once the inclement conditions worsened, to change the performance indoors with no excluded areas. They arrived at the captain's quarters, pleading their case. James had explained his situation vis-à-vis the concerns of seating for the black troops. Valenti said he would bow out if the captain relegated the black troops to a selected or segregated area. Confident of this peace accord, he and Valenti went directly to the captain.

"It's now or never, Vince." James looked at Vince, who knew that they would hold their ground and not capitulate one inch. "We may be making history here. They can't throw us all off the ship," a smiling James Hayes added.

Once inside the captain's quarters, James and Vince were asked to wait in the outer area. The captain didn't waste time and shaking hands with both James and Vince, asked what he could do for them. James would not be deterred and proceeded to speak.

"No separate areas, sir, please," James had insisted.

The captain, aware of the sensitive area of race, suggested that no designation would be in the offing, but that the black troops enter the theatre and sit together where they wanted. The captain, in an attempt to cut down on his smoking, had been chewing gum. When he saw the duo enter his office, he got up and reached out to them, discarding his gum in the trash.

James remembered the captain saying, "We got some yahoo boys on board that will never change their attitude. I don't need to tell you anymore. They will stay that way. But we have a common enemy to fight; I don't want to witness a problem in what should be an afternoon of entertainment." James made it clear that the black troops had insisted he make clear their intentions—they had put up with Jim Crow laws at home and in the living quarters of the ship, and they weren't about to give in on this issue. They wanted to sit where they felt comfortable.

The captain, aware of the sensitive nature, said he would not only welcome the event on their terms but also introduce the "first integrated band in the US troop ship." He added, "If I get hell from the upper brass in DC, so be it. I'm getting ready to retire. Once we smash the Germans in the trenches and hopefully all come home, maybe you can change things back home. Maybe some good will come out of this, who knows?"

James and Vince got the assurance that the captain was on their side, and they were now free to distribute and put up the flyers that were written with the date and time of the event. The captain was also thinking of his legacy. He liked the fact that he had done several runs of troop ships with few problems. This crossing was the best thanks to the efforts of Hayes and Valenti and the group. Instead of watching a silent movie, they could now have live entertainment. The captain knew it would resonate well with the other members of his crew. The show took on a life of its own. It became the talk of the ship.

With that, it was settled. James had done most of talking; Vince Valenti nodded approvingly when the captain gave the okay to move the event to the theatre. They would both report back to their respective groups and rehearse later that day. The rehearsal went over well. Allowed to use the theatre, they had the comedian, Suarez, also try out his routine.

Valenti, looking at Hayes, remarked, "He's lucky he doesn't get thrown overboard with this."

Suarez was very funny in the rehearsal, dishing the dirt on the staff and crew alike. No subject was off limits to him—the ship, the camouflage colors, the lack of women, the food. Oh! The food. It became a favorite item, including the quality of the food plus the dour faces of the staff assigned to give out the meals in cafeteria style in the beautiful dining room of the once luxury ship. His comedy routine, tried out on the music group, went over very well. Suarez was destined to become known.

The next day the talk on the ship was about the upcoming ragtime mix. The weather made the perfect excuse to hold the event in the theater. Blowing and drifting freezing winds clinched the decision. It had been brutal on board in early to late February in the North Atlantic. An outdoor event was out of the equation. Otherwise, it would have involved setting up a platform on deck for the band and singers and setting up chairs for the top brass. Utilizing the theater meant that all the legwork of setting up was done. The stage was large and used for the former German actors and singers. The seats were plush red velvet that complemented the equally lush red draperies on stage. The walls had murals of bygone mythical figures from Thor to the Greek god of the sea, Poseidon, to Athena and Midas.

By 2:00 p.m. there were no vacant seats left. The balconies with three tiers had been filled to capacity as well. The captain went onto stage to introduce this ad hoc musical group, pointing out this was the first time an integrated band ensemble and singers had assembled. "We're making history today, fellows." The captain was pleased that all had gone well and started by introducing each of the players and the hometowns where they were reared.

The comedian, Larry Suarez, opened up the events with his comedy routine. As he did in the rehearsal, his delivery was on target, joking about the close quarters, the odor of disinfectant in the bunk area, the few women on board, and the food. Following his quick-paced delivery, James got the musical events started with a few ragtime hits. Wes Morgan, Vince Valenti, and Tom Riker were the perfect trio as a backup to Hayes, Duggers, and St. Clair. Their voices soared, and the crowd loved the occasional digs they threw at each other. The hymns were saved for last, and they asked the crowd to join in singing "Amazing Grace."

The entire program took a little more than an hour and a half. With several announcements from the captain, he ended by pointing out the significance of the event. He mentioned, "We probably made history today. I'm proud of this ship, proud of the men and staff on this ship, and proud to be your captain."

With that, he received a standing ovation. When the captain asked for a big round of applause, another standing ovation was given. James, along with the testy Duggers and St. Clair, were all smiles. The music trio asked James to announce that when they arrived at the port of Brest, they would try to get some gigs before going off to deployment in the trenches. Knowing that black troops hadn't been given the opportunity to fight in the trenches in the Argonne Forest, the black soldiers knew they would probably remain either unloading cargo from ships coming into port or deployed as cleanup in the aftermath of battles—clearing the fields, taking the dead from the battle.

Duggers, ever the iconoclast, remarked, "We'll be looked at and sneered at like always. Glad you think things will change—they won't!"

Balancing a tight rope with Duggers and other blacks in the bunk wasn't easy. James knew of the catcalls, shoves, and provocations by some racist whites, but he knew he had to take the initiative and convince the most skeptical to take a plunge and at least try. That's what leadership was all about, and James Hayes did it well. Getting someone like Duggers, a talented and gifted voice, to join his group in an integrated ensemble was a landmark for him. Duggers even took a liking to the white musicians. It took a while, but as fellow artists, he appreciated their talents and it proved to be a hit. For James, it was a huge success. It united, however briefly, groups of men who came from various ethnic and geographic and religious backgrounds. They had a common cause of unity coupled with the reality of the soon-to-be conflagration in the French trenches. A moment to enjoy. A moment, however temporary, to forget about the anxieties of what might occur. Yes, James felt very good about the event—very good.

James Hayes returned to his assigned bunk after the concert to prepare for dinner, which would begin within the hour. Arriving at the bunk with Duggers and St. Clair, they were given another round of applause. His fellow bunkmates needed a respite from the drudgeries of the long time at sea. They were proud of what James Hayes had accomplished.

St. Clair, a quiet, laid-back Afro-Creole, had to speak up, and giving a wink to Hayes and a nod to Duggers, he proudly announced, "James pulled this off. He's the one that deserves the credit." Duggers, caught off guard a bit, smiled and nodded at St. Clair.

What had they done? A lot. They had captured the hearts of many of these men who had experienced so much hardship and injustice in their lives—men who never been outside the niche of their closed and restricted lives. The performance meant a great deal to them. They were grateful to James and the captain and the musicians willing to take a risk in an integrated ensemble. It was indeed a date that James would remember as well. He reached into his pocket and held his handkerchief, knowing fully well that his mom would be so pleased. He went into the washroom to freshen up. He was ready to chow down with his buddies. He felt pleased that he was able to pull off an event that few thought was possible. With a big smile on his face, he proceeded to the mess hall.

Along the way, he was met by his hometown boy, Jimmie Ray Owens. He was walking with a bespeckeled, slender, and tall guy. A big smile on Jimmy's face was followed by a hug. Jimmy pointed to the guy he was with and followed with an introduction to his friend, Ken Levinson of St. Louis. Levinson, of first-generation Russian Jewish immigrants whose family had fled the pogroms in Czarist Russia in 1905, was a bunkmate of Owens. He heard Owens tell others that he was friends with Hayes and came from the same Mississippi county.

Levinson approached Owens in the hope of meeting the now-famous James Hayes. Levinson had cousins who had settled in Paris and wanted to get up there once they landed in Brest before heading to the front or whenever they could get a leave of a few days. He approached Owens to arrange a meeting with Hayes and his group. Levinson wanted to introduce them to his uncle, who worked as a manager at a jazz club on the Left Bank. The club, Le Chat Noir (The Black Cat), became a favorite for many jazz devotees. It was a great spot where the likes of Gertrude Stein and her friend Alice B. Toklas often met. Ken's uncle, Marcel Levinson, was anxious to get raw talent and introduce it to the Paris night scene. It seemed to be the perfect mix. They welcomed new talent, and he felt he could get his cousin, Marcel, to get an engagement once he heard them.

When Jimmie Ray introduced Levinson to James, they instantly became friends. Despite their differences, they had a common love of music. They started talking about jazz, Scott Joplin, WC Handy, and the history of jazz. Levinson talked about the historic Columbian Exposition of 1893 that introduced jazz mainstream to white America.

Levinson neither sang nor played a musical instrument. But as a youngster, he heard a jazz ensemble. It was at another world's fair—the 1904 St. Louis Fair when he was just ten and fell in love with the music. He remembered the excitement from the crowd, the rhythm of the sound called jazz. He was mesmerized by the musicians and the magic that spewed from their instruments. Like the magical world's fair in his native St. Louis, the music set the pace for wide audience to appreciate the new sound. Soon spread with the advancement of technology, the music of jazz by 1917 could be heard on the phonograph.

The fact that Levinson loved jazz and wanted to help was a major plus for James. With the war always in the way, they started talking about a trek to Paris as soon as the Yanks could stop the "kraut advance." They had to wait for history to play out and the war to intervene. It wouldn't take long. The Germans were determined to make their last stand in the trenches. They went on the offensive and put all their efforts with the aim of winning by early 1918. Trench warfare would get only worse. And the Americans would be in the thick of it. But like all wars, the tide would turn, and the stronger and fresher troops would prevail. Paris and jazz and the music and the women would have to wait. They had to win in the trenches first. It would be achieved only by a constant barrage of guns, tanks, poison gas, and the deaths of many young men.

CHAPTER 16

The entry into Brest was on a cold, late February morning. The white troops on board were told that they would soon be sent to the front. With news of a renewed German advance on the front, the Allies were eager to get the fresh Yanks in the trenches and pull back the German advance. The Russians had surrendered to the Germans in early 1917 and now, in early 1918, all those troops on Eastern Front were moved on the Western Front. Their purpose was to defeat the French with a major offensive that would knock out France and have Britain plead for peace before the fresh arrival of American troops. In Russia, Czar Nicholas II and his entire family were executed at the orders of Lenin in early 1918. The horrors of the new communist regime in Moscow scared the rest of the Allies. The brutality of lining the royal house of Romanoff, shooting the czar, his wife, Alexandra, and their children, and dipping their remains in sulfuric acid was a clear indication that Lenin wanted to erase any trace of the regime. When Lenin took over, the czar had been forced to give up his power to the Bolsheviks. As part of the deal, Russia, an allied power of Britain, France, Italy, and the United States, gave up, surrendering to Imperial Germany at the Treaty of Brest-Livotsk. This gave the Germans a psychological boost in morale, and the Western Front was now a war zone, which was never witnessed by such bloodshed in the history of humankind. They knew that Wilson, who had a close reelection victory against a united Republican opponent, Governor

Charles Evans Hughes, would ask Congress for a war declaration once the Germans reneged on their Sussex Pledge. That pledge had stated that the Germans wouldn't torpedo neutral ships, such as United States. Once the Germans knew the election results in 1916 US presidential race, they knew they had to deal with the idealistic and messianic Wilson. Their fateful flaw was to think the Yanks couldn't get across the pond before the last-ditch German offensive on the Western Front. So the arrival of James Hayes and the troops would clearly turn the tide.

With that, all the Germans troops on the Eastern Front would now make one final and decisive trust into the Western Front in the French and Belgium farmlands. The strategy in Berlin was that the Americans couldn't get their troops to the front until spring, 1918. But the American Expeditionary Force, led by John J. Pershing, was able to get thousands of Americans to the front by early 1918. With the arrival of *Leviathan's* fourteen thousand troops and other American troop ships coming in late February 1918, it was a do-or-die moment for the Germans. The Central Powers, led by Germany, wanted to beat France and force Britain to the peace table as quickly as possible. The Americans would be too late to do anything. It almost worked, but it was not to be. But it came at a very heavy price.

This scenario indeed almost succeeded. The Germans were fierce fighters, and their use of mustard gas scared the hell out of the Allies. First used by the Germans in 1915 in Belgium at the Battle of Ypes, it was a form of chlorine gas. It would burn the throat, resulting in an edema of the lungs and agonizing death by asphyxiation. The acrid air stunk of the potent gas, whose mist was like a low-hanging cloud. It also blinded the unfortunate Allied troops in the wretched trenches when the cloud of gas got in their eyes. And it got only worse. By 1917, the Germans were now substituting mustard gas for the chlorine. Imagine being in the trenches and a warning comes out to put on the gas mask. Not able to secure their gas masks on time, an Allied soldier would be gasping for air and die from the effects of such a brutal attack.

The fast-moving mortars of artillery also saw men died by the thousands as exploding canisters met their mark. Riflemen also fought hand-to-hand combat, and the tanks would roll over many in the trenches. Coupled with the new advances of warfare, such as the machine gun, tanks, and the dreaded German submarine, the Teutonic might was not to be taken lightly.

This was the situation when James Hayes and all the other troops landed in Brest. It was a brutal war, the likes of which the world had never witnessed. It brought nothing but death and heartache and stalemate along the trenches in France. Added to the dreadful mix was the combination of log-watered trenches that brought about trench fever and mud during the rainy season. The resulting climatic challenges made many men sick, suffering from trench foot. Trench foot, not taken care of in time, would lead to amputations due to spread of gangrene. Even worse was the presence of rodents that fed on the dead and the constant mosquitoes after the summer rain. Added to this were millions of flies eating off the dead before the medics could attend to them. One British medic remarked, "This has to be as close to hell on earth as anything imagined."

Life in the trenches was exacerbated by the barbed wire that entangled and maimed many of the men on both sides. Erected by the French along the Maignot Line, it backfired when many Allied troops became entangled in the barbed wire, causing cuts and death. Dead horses also used to pull supplies and armament were scattered throughout.

The area separating the trenches on both sides was known as no-man's land. It was the area that was prized to take over and claim for one's country. It was there that most of the men fell in hand-to-hand combat.

Such was the state of war in early 1918. Both the Allies and the Central Powers had experienced four long years of carnage. They were exhausted. Their ranks were dwindling, and unrest was evident in the countries affected by the horrific loss of life. But the Germans and their allies, the Austrians, Turks, and Bulgarians, were determined to succeed in the last great offensive. Back home, the German people were feeling the effects of the British blockade. Scattered rioting and demonstrations resulted in major German cities from Berlin to Frankfurt to

Hamburg. With the arrival of the Americans on ships, such as the *Leviathan*, the tide would turn decisively. It was just what the German high command in Berlin was wishing to avoid.

The black troops were assigned to unload the cargo and stay in port and remain there for next three months while the white troops would head into the trust of the battles in the trenches and face no-man's land in the northern French forest. Day after day, the black troops were assigned to unload the cargo, clean up the ships after additional troops arrived, and fumigate all the quarters before the ships returned to the United States and shuttle more troops to the front. Others worked in the supply room, making sure the troops had the right ammo and clothes to withstand the devastating damp and cold in the trenches. Working as service employees while others went off to battle made some of the black troops angry. Among them was James Hayes, who had distinguished himself as a very accurate marksman and would be on the front if not for the color of his skin. He too began to think the way the more blunt-talking Duggers did.

James and his fellow black troops started getting antsy and wanted to contribute to the war effort. *I can shoot as well as any white man*, James would say to himself, occasionally glancing at Duggers, thinking he was for real and knew the deal. But James felt soon that the Ninety-Third Division that he and the other black troops were in would be called to the front. He knew the French wanted the black troops to fight right alongside the French troops. The Germans had made some progress, and the fighting was as fierce and brutal, with tremendous loss of lives. James wanted out of this situation in Brest harbor. He knew that the captain of the *Leviathan* had recommended that the musical ensemble that had performed extent their talent to the harried troops by performing at hospitals and in venues whenever needed. Yet there were other issues. Logistics and politics always got in the way.

The Americans who didn't want to fight with the blacks would be spared being alongside black soldiers.

Duggers, upon hearing this, said to Hayes, "What did you expect—a red carpet welcome? Make the world safe for democracy—such crap! Wilson allows segregation, allows that racist movie *Birth of a Nation*." Duggers shook his head, laughing sarcastically. Making sure he got his message across, his voice rising, he concluded by saying, "We would rather make Georgia, Mississippi, Alabama, Georgia, and the Carolinas safe for the Negro—such bullshit, pure bullshit!"

James knew how Franklin Duggers and the other men felt. *Duggers is right on with this*. Indeed, back in the United States, there were thirty-eight documented lynchings in 1917, followed by fifty-eight in 1918. The KKK was back in action all the way from Texas to New England. The Klan also targeted Catholics and Jews, questioning their loyalty.

And in the US Army, segregation followed the soldiers. Some white officers reserved the hottest shell holes and filthiest jobs for blacks. This prejudice didn't end at water's edge. As a result, it was determined that the black Ninety-Second and Ninety-Third Divisions would fight with the more tolerant French troops. The French wanted help, and it didn't matter to them what color the soldier was. Combat troops were needed as the spring of 1918 gave way to summer. It was rumored that the high command in the French and American divisions argued as to what to do with combat black troops.

Finally, a decision was made. Indeed, some 350,000 African-Americans served with the US Army on the Western Front. A clear one-fifth would ultimately involve in combat. They were 3 percent of the American Expeditionary Force and 2 percent of battlefield fatalities. At first these same black troops who worked as stevedores at Brest harbor united with American General Pershing's blessing to receive several regiments of black combat troops.

James Hayes and the other black troops making up the Ninety-Third Division finally were ordered to the front in May, 1918. As part of the Ninety-Third, they were never fully equipped. Some of the Americans, their obvious prejudice apparent, indicated that they would not fight alongside black troops.

Like in the old Jim Crow South, the white and black troops would be separated. The French command wanted every available man who would could to serve in the trenches. French officials decided that the black troops could serve with them. Several of the senior white officers didn't like the arrangement with the French high command. The war, however, dictated that fresh troops from America could turn the tide of war. The Germans, like the Allies, were tired of war. There were more rumors by spring that cities in Germany were feeling the effects of the British blockade on the high seas, despite the ever-present danger of the German submarines. Food was becoming scare in the German shops, from the small towns to the big cities. There were reports that some Germans wanted peace negotiations. The French and Americans wanted to seize the moment by crushing the German offensive in the trenches.

An all-black unit, the 369th, soon teamed up as well. Formed at Camp Whitman in upstate New York, most of their men were from New York City. They quickly became known as the Harlem Hellfighters. Divided into three battalions, the Fifteenth Regiment was sent south to Spartanburg, South Carolina. In one episode, two black soldiers were refused service when attempting to buy a newspaper from the local store that serviced the soldiers—the white soldiers. Two white soldiers came to the aid of the soldiers. They were from the all-white Twenty-Seventh Regiment. Soon, a directive was sent to the shop owner, "If you don't serve black soldiers, you can close and leave town."

The 369th eventually ended up in France along the front. Issued French weapons, like the soldiers of the Ninety-Second and Ninety-Third Divisions, their experience in the war became famous. Unlike the incident in South Carolina, they were subjected to harassment by white, racist soldiers and were put under the command of French Army. Some American commanders didn't want to have them fight under their command, thus the reason for the French weapons, helmets, and command. This duality of acceptance by some and virulent racism by others became part of the black experience in the summer and fall of 1918.

Combined with French colonial units from Africa, James Hayes and the black troops wore old, blue American uniforms, some dating back to the time of the US Civil War and Spanish-American War. They were given Remington Arms rifles rather than the standard Springfield M1903 rifles or the Enfield M1917. These Buffalo soldiers, as they were called back home by Native Americans in the nineteenth century, would help to end the war. Many of these Southern black troops could fire a weapon and didn't need much training. That many had learned to shoot game back home would be a major advantage on the front.

When James and his men from the Ninety-Third got to the front, they were joined with the 369th infantry regiment. Known as the Harlem Freedom Fighters, they would go on to be on the front line for the next six months, longer than any other African American regiment in the war. The battles were raging during the spring and summer of 1918 in the Meuse-Argonne region. Hayes and his comrades were quickly in the thick of battle in the trenches.

CHAPTER 17

By the end of May, James Hayes and the other black troops were in the thick of the fighting. He and his Ninety-Third Division would be joined by the French Sixteenth Division in the Meuse-Argonne Forest. This was the middle of the German offensive. Many of the French Sixteenth were from North and West Africa serving in the French military. A sense of the Diaspora of the black soldier bonded these men despite the language barriers. The presence of these soldiers gave the black American soldiers a much-needed lift after being treated poorly with menial tasks in the port of Brest. Several times, black soldiers were singled out for no reason in Brest whenever supplies weren't loaded as fast as expected or wanted. Singled out for racist treatment, they were often viewed as a threat to white authority. Reports of court martials among black troops were common. These same soldiers had done the work that no one wanted to perform.

Duggers, ever the skeptic, angry, and militant of the group that Hayes was part of, remarked candidly, "I don't want to stagger under heavy boxes." He and the others had, up to now, worked the docks at Brest. When asked what he expected to do, he quickly responded, "I am a soldier, as good as any white man. I want a gun on my shoulder and the chance to get to the front. This bullshit should stop now!"

And Franklin Duggers soon got his wish. With the German advance ever a threat, they were finally sent off to the front. Duggers was correct that being treated as second-class citizens at home transcended to black troops here—except for the people of Brest and the French high command. They needed every able body and wanted to include black troops.

Duggers often remarked to Hayes, "I go into town and get a few rations—I like hot French bread right out of the oven. The nice old lady always smiles and gives me a nice slab of butter. I get treated better here without the looks and sneers I get at the base. So, yeah, I'm a soldier, and I get to do the job. I can do the job!"

The rigors of combat and labor challenged all who fought, be they Allied or Central Powers. War is war, and the horrors of it soon started to take a toll. It affects the emotional and physical stamina of anyone who has to endure the constant threat of death. The constant shelling, barrage of flying missiles, poison gas, and hand-to-hand combat dragged on throughout the spring and summer of 1918. And for what? A small patch of land to defend and drive an enemy back. At what cost? It was all about death and destruction. The land was depleted of its trees, its soil blown up, and the ground saturated with poison. And the death. Not just ordinary, everyday passings. No! Death didn't care about color, rank, social standing, age, or looks. It became the great equalizer, as it always does. It affected everyone involved. No getting around it. Soon the black troops fighting for an America that didn't totally accept them gave their full weight and effort to the cause.

By September, the fighting raging, the war become personal. It would a day that would be etched in the mind of James for the rest of his life. It would affect him like no other.

It all began early, shortly after dawn. With little sleep for the past two nights, the German advance had been relentless. Many casualties resulted from the constant barrage of fighting on the front. For the Germans, it was a now-or-never moment. It would all come to a head on September 12.

That morning, the constant din of the guns and canisters and barrage of surface-to-air trajectories made the men in the foxhole very aware of the severity of the enemy offensive.

Fighting in the trenches on September 12, a canister of poison gas came screeching into the trench. James had just remarked to Duggers, who was to the left of him, "You got to give these damn Germans credit. They're not about to give up."

He gave James a smile. But something wasn't right. Just after finishing his sentence, an exploding rocket-propelled weapon made the scary, loud whizzing sound and hit the trench hard to the left of James Hayes. James, although shaken up and momentarily grounded, was able to get up. He had his gas mask on, as did the others in the trench. He brushed off the excess dirt that had found its way in his hair and into his loosely wrapped gas mask. He glanced over at Duggers. The noise from the machine guns and exploding canisters muffled his voice. Soon, he was yelling at Duggers, who was still.

The canister had temporarily blinded James, and he kept shouting out to Duggers, "You okay?" He got no response and again inquired and looked to the left, only to find his buddy Franklin Duggers dead with his gas mask on.

It was a horrific sight for James. Franklin Duggers's eyes were opened wide with no expression; Duggers had received a direct hit and died instantly. Blood was seeping from his upper right side. Hayes yelled at the top of his lungs, "We need a medic now, right now."

Yet he knew that Duggers hadn't made it. Despite the incessant noise of the continuing warfare, James took off his helmet and mask and grabbed his dead friend and shouted, "Somebody help! Help! Speak to me, speak to me! I'm not going to let this pass. You, of all people, dead. No. No. What's going on—what's going on! Not you! Oh God, what the hell just happened?" James looked around and shouted, "We need someone here. We need someone here." At that, James buried his soiled face in his hands and wept openly.

James was soon surrounded by several other soldiers in the trench, including Beau St. Clair. James shook his head and said repeatedly, "I just never thought he would be the one to go. It's not fair—it's not fair. Goddamn!"

St. Clair grabbed James and held him for what seemed a long time, yet was just a few seconds. "James, my God, he's gone!"

Medics quickly arrived and knowing that James and Franklin Duggers were close friends, said, "There's nothing we can do here." One look at Duggers confirmed what the seasoned medics knew—Franklin was beyond help.

"I'm sorry." The medic gently touched James, adding, "I have to go. We had quite a hit. Too many damaged bodies." With that, it was confirmed that Franklin Duggers had become a casualty of the Great World War. Far from home, his death, like thousands of others, would go unnoticed, except for a poor woman in Detroit.

James looked about the trench and realized that the hit that killed Duggers had also hit the mark with several others dead. A whistle signaled that the offense had temporarily lulled. It was time to assess the damage and administer to those in need. Disoriented, Beau got him to break away from Duggers's body and move onto higher ground.

The brief lull allowed the triage unit to get the most severely wounded out of the trench and onto a stretcher to a nearby tent serving as a hospital. His mind preoccupied in a surreal panorama, he witnessed two other medics take Duggers's body away. In all, four were killed that early morning, and within ten minutes, another alarm sounded for the men to don their gas masks. What seemed like an eternity but lasted just three minutes was a barrage of bullets, flying missiles brought additional death and injuries to the already jaded unit. The war had indeed come home for James Hayes. His closest friend dead, plus the carnage around him, found him reaching into his pocket and grabbing his mom's handkerchief. Now soiled, he held it as a pious congregant might hold a rosary or cross. In his deepest grief, the handkerchief linked him to a comfort zone. It represented a link to back home. He thought of his parents and his brother. Within a few minutes, the all-clear signal was given, and the medics reappeared to retrieve the dead and take care of the wounded. The action was swift but the black troops held their ground, and their constant barrage back at the Germans helped put them on the run. It was a moment of mixed emotions for James.

James looked about trying to absorb what happened. The war had indeed hit home for him. *He died for what? To go back to the same bullshit* he had before? These damn Germans did nothing to us personally. What a world we live in! I go back to Mississippi; I'll still be a nobody. All this reading to better my English—Duggers was right. I'm just another throwaway—that's all I am to those assholes. Duggers, you were right. God, you were right. We're like the lepers—lepers from the Bible. Cast aside and avoided. Like lepers, we're looked on differently. They only use us. They only want us to fight and get back to what was. No! I've had enough. Only used when they need us. Yes, Duggers, you were right, you were so right! Hayes walked back with Beau to the barracks. They passed by several of the white soldiers on the next trench. Aware of the direct hit, several went up to Hayes. He was known from the concert. Two of them walked up and nodded. Hayes knew that gesture, however fleeting, was an acceptance of a job well done.

When he got to the barracks, the totality of it hit him. He went over to Duggers's locker. James and Franklin Duggers made a pact—that if one fell in combat, the other would write a letter to his next of kin. Beau St. Clair also was in on the pact. James had Duggers's address to his mom in Detroit. He knew the army would notify her via telegram, but he wanted to write the letter while emotions were still raw. Beau asked James to write, as he felt James was closer and would do a better job.

He wrote telling Mae Duggers that her son's insistence on respect and demanding change would stay with him and be a catalyst for justice. In part, James was making a confessional. Time had shown him that he had to take action. He would take up the mantle from Duggers and use it for change. In his condolences letter, written two days after the death of Franklin Duggers, he wrote, "Your son taught me much. He taught me to question authority. He was always quick to ask why whenever an order was directed at the black troops and not at the white ones. He knew that changes had to come. He didn't want to wait. He enriched me. A part of me died with him because I depended on him for advice and for a quick joke. I'll miss him terribly, but I want you to know this—your son was loved by not only the colored troops but also many of the white troops. He was the real deal. He was major part of our musical group. When we performed, his voice soared, and it united this crazy country separated by race. What's the matter with the world? I don't know, but I do know the world was a better place thanks to your son. His voice, his smile, his anger, and his love will never, never leave me."

James put down his pen. He was overwhelmed. He hadn't slept well since the death of Duggers. He internalized, asking what they were doing here. True, they wanted to contribute to the war effort—not so much to immerse themselves into the battle but to show that they could excel. And excel they did. James was pleased that his self-taught grammar and writing gave him the skills that he hadn't acquired in school. He was proud to be self-taught. He was proud to speak and write well. But he couldn't quite come to terms with this situation. He would indeed use the tragic death of Franklin Duggers to inform and educate anyone, anytime. He didn't think of his now-reduced singing group and the dream of going to Paris to perform at the Chat Noir. All that meant nothing to him now.

Beau St. Clair and the trio musical ensemble, led by Valenti, asked the commander if they could perform at the field hospital. Beau wanted James to use it as a tribute to the fallen Duggers and others. At first reluctant to comply, he finally gave in, and the resulting tribute to the fallen at the Argonne was a fitting remembrance of a unique, angry, and right-on man like Duggers. Beau remarked that, despite the absence of Franklin Duggers's basso profundo voice, the now duet of Beau St. Clair and the soaring voice of James Hayes could still come through. James's voice never sounded better, and with tears streaming down his cheeks, he soared with "How Great Thy Art." By the end of the tribute, both black and white troops were on their feet.

Beau remarked to James, "He did it, man. Franklin would have loved it. You did it, man."

James, not knowing for sure what St. Clair meant, asked, "Did what?"

"You showed them what we've been through. You gave Duggers dignity. You did it. When they asked you to say something, I liked that you said that we don't forget but move on. We won't give up—not on this war and our own war back home. I think they got it, James." The normally quiet St. Clair articulated, in his own way, the fact that Duggers's life was eulogized not only in song but also in his demands for justice. James Hayes did indeed perform. But Beau wanted to say more; he had to.

"James, look around. Nobody ain't gonna ever say we didn't do our job. Nobody will. They know who's real, for sure, James, for sure! Duggers united this group better than any concert." Beau was right on target. The normally taciturn Creole from New Orleans hit a home run with assessment. For the first time since Duggers's death, James was smiling. He suddenly got it.

After the service for Franklin Duggers and the seven others who fell that day in the other trenches, nobody would speak of the colored troops as ineffective, lax, and not prepared. Duggers had, in death, united the troops. It took a misfortune of war from the most outspoken, angry, and skeptical of all to bring unity, however briefly, to the men on the front that afternoon.

What resulted is that men such as Hayes, Duggers, and St. Clair, all members of the Ninety-Third Division, had fought as part of France's Fourth army. They made history. So it was that a tense truce resulted when the black troops were separated from the white Americans and teamed up with the French and their black colonial fighters. It was the summer of 1918, and the presence of the Ninety-Second and Ninety-Third Division did not go unnoticed. Even General John J. "Black Jack" Pershing of the American Expeditionary Force when informed of the success in holding the front and pushing back the German advance remarked, "I cannot commend too highly the spirit shown among colored troops who exhibited the fine capacity for quick training and eagerness for the most dangerous work." It was an endorsement from the head of the US Army who saw first-hand the accomplishments of the troops under the most dangerous conditions.

The black troops in the middle of the German offensive held their ground, refused to give in, and continued the relentless attack. With the addition of the Harlem Hellfighters, they joined up with the French to drive the Germans back from the advance and overtook their trenches. James Hayes was part of this unit. One would go on to make history.

In one cold, damp night raid by the Germans, Henry Johnson of the Hellfighters 369th became a hero when he held off an entire German raiding party. Using only a pistol and bolo knife and his bare fists, he killed four Germans and wounded several others of the raiding party numbering twenty-four. In still another significant raid, on September 25, the 369th with Hayes and Johnson captured the village of Sechault and continued fighting at both Battles of Bellau Wood and Chateau-Thierry. One of these actions allowed a wounded comrade to escape and resulted in the capture of stockpiles of German arms. Henry Johnson would soon be a hero. He and James were leaders, and the word quickly got back to main headquarters.

When hearing of the heroic exploits of Johnson, former President Theodore Roosevelt remarked, "Johnson was one of the five bravest Americans to serve in the World War." This was the same president who had charged up San Juan Hill and routed the Spanish in Cuba twenty years earlier during the Spanish-American War. Roosevelt knew what he talking about—a military man, leader, and president, his comments meant so much.

But like the now-deceased Duggers, Johnson was the subject of racial abuse. James Hayes remembered the sneers he and Johnson received from some white troops who questioned their bravery. Many were, no doubt, jealous, not wanting a black man to be cited by the former president among others for their service "above and beyond the call of duty."

Johnson would be awarded the *Croix de Guerre* from a very grateful French government. In his native Albany, New York, a street is named for him in the Arbor Hill Section, not far from the capitol building. He had been employed in the menial job of rail station redcap porter at Union Station in downtown Albany just down State Street from the state capitol. He had carried many bags of both corrupt and legit lawmakers on their way down the Hudson on the trains heading to New York. With the completion of Grand Central in 1913, he and the other porters had worked long hours with little pay. Today the city of Albany recognized one of their own and his outstanding contribution to the war effort. In addition to the street named in his honor, the US Post Office at 747 Broadway in Albany was renamed for him. In 2007, a charter school in Albany was renamed for him. His granddaughter was present at the ceremony.

Thanks to the actions of men like Johnson and Hayes, raiding parties continued to do damage to the frazzled German line, and soon many of the Germans were in retreat. By late October, it was just a matter of time.

CHAPTER 18

James Hayes had one of those dreams again on the night of November 10. It was the faceless angel with the white dress. A red sash around her mid-section, she smiled at him. She had beckoned to him, motioning with her hands for him to come up to a stage she was on. She seemed to be performer—perhaps a singer. The room was smoky, the haze of smoke making it difficult to see where he was. But she was there, glowing, radiant, and warm.

Like most dreams, it was flashes. But this dream had recurred for many months from the time he was stationed at Camp Funston, aboard the ship, and even when in the barracks at Brest for the three months there and now here on the front. With the death of Duggers still a problem for him that kept him up some nights, he saw it as an omen. What kind of omen—good or bad? The faceless woman in the white dress was on stage—was she a source of good? James Hayes hoped so.

Approximately at 5:00 a.m., a commotion broke out throughout the barracks. It aroused James, who quickly got dressed and ask, "What's going on?"

"Get your butts up, now! The friggen war is over! The Germans are surrendering today. Yes, today. It's all over. We're gonna go home! It's time to celebrate. We're gonna go home! Let's go, men!"

One of the men went from bunk to bunk, hitting the steel posts with a blade. This was followed by a few of the men from the mess hall banging on pots. The deafening noise brought about a lot of laughter.

One of the very sound sleepers, a short, slender solider from Ohio, had a rude awakening when the pot-banging soldier went up to his ear and let loose. He nearly hit his head on the upper bunk when he jumped up to find extended laughter.

"Get up! The krauts are surrendering. You're going home, boy!" the loud soldier grabbed the petite sleeper by one hand and pulled him out of the bed. These scenes no doubt were duplicated at the white bunks and all the places, be they Allied or Central soldiers. The chaotic scene was replete with hugs, shouts, hand-slapping, and singing.

James went over to his friend Beau St. Clair, who was already dressed at 5:15 a.m. "We got this rotten war over." Beau gave his friend and fellow singer a faint smile, knowing that not all of the men were going home. "Yeah, I know what you're thinking—wishing old Duggers was here." Beau looked at James with a look that demanded a response.

Never one to mince words, James was quick to respond, "You know, when we went through his personal stuff, I found a keychain with his initials on it. I gave all his valuables to be sent home—pictures, comb, and a few other things. But I was told to keep the keychain—it has his initials on it, and it's something to remember him by."

"A keepsake—right?" Beau asked.

"Yes, just like my handkerchief. I'll keep it for as long as I can. Now, I have Duggers's keychain too. He told me to keep it if anything happened to him." Looking at St. Clair, James wanted to ask him something personal.

"Listen, Beau. You wanna get home right away, right?"

"Hell, yes. Don't you?" Beau was surprised at the suggestion that he not go home.

"I wanna get up to Paris. I wanted Duggers, you, and me to go and see if would get a gig …"

"It's over, man. Look, you can go. I got to get back to New Orleans. Got family and a girl that has been writing me more often. Gotta get back, just got to. You dig?" Beau's voice was getting shrill. James knew he hit a raw nerve.

"I'm not going back to Mississippi—not just yet. Want to see what

Paris is all about. Want to see some of those clubs, meet some of those girls …"

"Hold on, count me out." Beau was trying to make sense of this. Despite all the euphoria and noise and others coming up and slapping their backs and hands, he had to make a valid point to his friend. He had to get this off his chest. This was as good a time as any.

"I would think about it, but we're no longer a group without Franklin. You know this and you know you have a great voice, and damn, you should go up there and drink that wine, meet those women, and sing in one of them joints. Do it, James, do it! Besides, you got that voice. It's unique, my man. You the star, not me, not me. Duggers and me were your back up. You the man, James. You the man." James Hayes looked at his friend, laughing aloud, showing his pearly white teeth. He felt good and appreciated Beau's candor.

Beau St. Clair was at least three inches shorter than his friend. He was prematurely bald already at twenty-one, had a twitch in his left eye, and paled in comparison to James. James, tall, good-looking, with a thick mane of hair that complemented his fine physique, always attracted the women both at home and at Camp Funston and now in France. St. Clair knew that James was unattached and would have to get to Paris. It was something he always talked about. For Beau, going home was the most important item. Had Duggers lived, he would have gone up on leave and tried to get a gig. But now it was different. Yet, Beau knew that James's fine voice plus his physical presence would be a plus. Deep down, he felt he could go it alone. He didn't need him. Beau knew this and wanted, in a most sensitive way, explain that James would be a hit, even had Duggers survived.

James suggested that they go outside, as the celebratory mood was exacerbated by the ever-increasing din of noise and shouts. Once outside, both black and white, French, Brits, and the staff working on the base joined the throng of revelers. The war to end all wars ended that day at 11:00 a.m. on the eleventh day of the eleventh month—November. From that day forward, it would be known as Armistice Day, as the day the Germans laid down their arms. The date, November

11, would eventually be used to commemorate the contributions of all service men and women in the armed forces. Now known as Veterans Day, it remains an important tribute for our country and is celebrated throughout the world. Exhausted by the constant barrage of ever-increasing fresh Yanks from across the pond, the mighty blockade by Britain had made its mark. What resulted in major German cities were food riots and raids on bakeries and meat markets and a plea to the Kaiser to surrender. With the German people starving and the enormous loss of life that all troops experienced, they had had enough of war. The Kaiser fled to Holland in exile, and the German government collapsed under the weight of the demands of the people. Now, that it was over, the soldiers could dust off their civilian clothes and get ready to be deployed and head home. It was indeed a special moment.

Like any man fighting in the horrors of the trenches, James showed his excitement by joining in the crowd. The few females working there—nurses in the infirmary, kitchen mess hall staff, and the local women—all were in rare demand as the troops began an orgy of kissing and dancing to no music and singing. One of the local French women came up to James and kissed him European style on both cheeks. No more than twenty, he had seen her in the infirmary working. The fact that a very serious pandemic of influenza that had already wrecked lives and killed thousands was creeping into the barracks was a major concern. As a result, many local volunteers were helping those affected. James had heard that Jimmy Ray was in the infirmary just yesterday. He wanted to stop by and see how he was doing. But at the moment, he wanted to enjoy the affections of the young ladies.

In halting English, the petite, black-haired local said to James, "Thank you so much. Merci."

James gave her a kiss on the cheek, and she smiled broadly and waved as she joined a few of her female coworkers from the infirmary. Looking on, Beau had to add, "I told you—any woman, any woman."

Joined together in victory, they forget about the horrors, injustices, and drama that made this war so unique. At least, now on the winning side, they could leave it to the politicians to decide what to do with the vanquished. Black or white, British or French or Italian or African colonial troops, they were united albeit for a brief time.

Walking up to them was Ken Levinson, his right arm in a sling. Levinson had shrapnel wound his upper arm and had been in the infirmary for a few days. He came up to Hayes and St. Clair, a nervous smile on his face. "I'm glad this is over."

"What happened, Ken?" James wanted to get the lowdown on his situation.

"I was one of the lucky one, James. A piece of shrapnel hit me in the upper bicep. Your friend Jimmie Ray was in the same trench with me. He was okay but started to feel sick that same night."

"Did he get gassed?"

"No, it's this damn influenza. He's confined in the infirmary. They wouldn't let me see him. Said his fever was too high. This bug going around is getting serious. I want to see Jimmie Ray—maybe today."

"Damn." James, looking at Ken, asked, "I hear about this flu being so bad. Is he going to make it?"

"I hope so, I hope so. I understand his fever is down, but a few guys have already died. It's so unfair, isn't it? I mean, going through all this only to get this bug."

"Life's unfair, Ken."

"Yes, yes it is. We lost so many, so many. By the way, now this mess is over, I'm going up to Paris. Please let me know if you're still interested in going to Paris. Really want to see my uncle. I never met him. My dad writes to him. I know his club is one of the best jazz joints in Paris." Ken wanted a response. His nudged James with his good arm. He still had residual pain. The shrapnel had been totally cleaned out of his arm. It was taking a little time to heal. Ken's aim was clearly to get James on board for the trip to Paris.

"It's not on my mind right now. Do you want to see Jimmie Ray and then we'll talk, okay?" James gently patted Ken's good arm, and he and Beau left, the crowd growing larger and getting louder by the moment.

Levinson was at the memorial for Duggers and the others and knew it was time not to discuss any gigs or any venue at the moment. Today, however, was a good day. The war over. He wanted to make sure his friend James would come to Paris with him. He had already made plans!

Once the festivities died down, James went back to his bunk thinking of his family. He had a letter dated October 14 from Ms. Hurley, who wrote for James's mother. He reached into his pocket to get out his friend—the handkerchief. James was grateful that, in the letter, Jane Hurley indicated that all was well and that the family was getting by. Looking at the nicely folded handkerchief, he wondered what his family—especially his mom—would think if he went up to Paris. What if he liked the city? Finding it to his liking, he thought, *What if it's for me?* To extend his stay or not. Well, he would soon find out.

He thought of Charles Atwood. In the last letter, he found out that his wife had given birth to an eight-pound, six-ounce girl. He was happy that Charles didn't have to endure the horrors witnessed by Hayes in the trenches and the overall experience overseas. The war made him grow up fast. He was ready, even at age twenty, to face any eventuality. Mississippi was a far-off place. He had confidence that he could, if he wanted, make a go at it in Paris. He decided to take Ken up on his offer. He would go to Paris.

Paris! Even the sound of it sounded so alluring. He had heard about the clubs, the women, the food, the wine, and the music and the fact that he could sit in any bistro. He could enjoy a bite without having to confine himself to a segregated table.

He had gone to the makeshift library adjacent to the mess hall. He looked at the pictures of the city—the Eiffel Tower, Notre Dame, the parks, the Louvre, the many squares—and he liked what he saw. He also read up on the famous *Moulin Rouge*. "Maybe, just maybe, I'll perform there."

But he cast aside the idea and folded the handkerchief in his pocket as Beau said, "Let's get some chow. With all this excitement, I need something in my belly."

Looking at Beau, he nodded, and the two headed to the mess hall, James adding, "I'm going to Paris. Come with me." A nod from Beau was a clear signal that he too had taken to Ken's offer. Right now, they were two young, excited hungry men.

"Okay, I'm game." With that, they headed to the mess hall. It was living up to its name. Although the news of the armistice was dying down, the mess hall was louder and more raucous than ever. James sat down next to one of his Harlem Hellfighters from Pittsburgh, and Beau slid up beside him in elongated, collapsible table used often in cafeterias, church halls, and bingo parlors. They ate a hearty breakfast of bacon, eggs over easy with grits, and French bread toasted and dripping in butter.

"The eggs aren't dripping today—the chef got it right," James said as he picked up his coffee cup.

With a strong *café au lait*, the black troops, as well as the white ones in the other mess hall, enjoyed the savors of victory. Before long, music broke out. Someone shouted, "Brother Hayes, when you finish chowing down, give us a song."

Applause erupted, and James stood up and said, "After we eat, let's all join in." Shouts of, "Yeah, that's right, got to do it" could be heard as James enjoyed eggs that were edible and not runny, and he broke out in a big smile. And James delivered.

He and Beau stood and began to sing "Swing Low, Sweet Chariot." A large segment of the crowd joined in, attracting the white troops passing by and hearing the loud chorus. A few ventured in and joined in the singing without any problem. Soon, more mundane tunes a la Scott Joplin jazzed up the impromptu performance. Within a few minutes, one of the men, Dwight Welles of Oklahoma, brought along his banjo. He asked James if he knew the words to "Easy Winners" and "Muslin Rag." Both James and the New Orleans native, Beau, did, and despite the absence of Duggers, they hit it off with the troops. Once again, James Hayes, the son of a poor sharecropper, displayed his strength through his talents. James felt confident. If his fellow troops like him as a performer, perhaps he could make it in the music world.

Within a few days, notices were given out for troop shipment. Some of the troops, such as the Ninety-Second and Ninety-Third and those attached to the 369th Harlem Hellfighters had been given a leave for two weeks. Most of the troops decided to go to Paris with their army stipend and see the sites of the City of Lights. Paris! Just the sound of it. They'd had enough of this killing. They were young, virile, and ready to see and do things. The war was over. What did all this mean?

They had killed an enemy with which they had no beef. It meant being proud and yet facing the reality. It meant getting away from the fear and threats from an experience back home. It also meant a chance to see life. Life! Seeing a city full of energy, action, music, dance, fine restaurants, museums, great cathedrals, and being free. Being free. To James Hayes, it was not just a chance to show his talents. It was a once-in-a-lifetime event that could alter his entire life. He knew that his decision was final. He didn't need any additional coaxing from Levinson. He would go to Paris with or without Beau and the backup group of musicians. He would go—he would definitely go!

CHAPTER 19

Paris! At long last, James Hayes arrived in the city in January 1919. In his entourage were Ken Levinson and Beau St. Clair. They left the barracks after visiting Jimmie Ray in the infirmary, who survived a bad bout with the pandemic influenza virus. Jimmie Ray would be going home for further medical treatment, as the flu bug sapped him of energy. He nearly lost his life. James was glad to stop by the infirmary and see his now-emaciated friend before leaving for Pairs.

James, at the urging of Levinson, got St. Clair to go to Paris for a few weeks before heading back to New Orleans. The musical trio of Valenti, Riker, and Morgan opted out and headed back to the United States. Valenti had a sick mother, Riker was scheduled to be married in the new year, and Morgan had a less-serious scrape with influenza and was eager to get back home.

Levinson was hopeful that his never-seen uncle would receive James and get him a chance to perform at the Chat Noir. Levinson, ever the optimist, remarked, "James, you'll be a hit. They'll love you—I'm willing to bet on it." Other notable jazz clubs in Paris were Le Grand Duc, Chez Florence, and Bricktop. James could always audition at those venues if he didn't make it at Ken's uncle's place. But, Ken Levinson knew from the tone of his uncle's letters that the club was looking for new and raw talent.

Ken Levinson wanted to expose James by bringing him to his uncle's club, which was one of the most frequented by many Americans and lovers of jazz. With the war over, he felt the time was ripe for new talent. And he was right on target.

Seeing Paris for the first time for anyone is a unique experience. The grand city, like the elegant lady she is, beckons you to challenge her at every level. The seductive nature of this lady spews forth in every corner. The city is full of life, noise, movement, and traffic. And people—oh the French. Once smitten by her, it's hard to avoid the lure. Captivating with the uniqueness that only Paris offers, one becomes a part of it. Songs, musicals on New York's famed Broadway, and the gastronomic delights of the food made it then, as now, a *grande dame*.

From the bistros aligning the Champs Elyse to the grand boulevards and manicured parks adjacent to the Eiffel Tower to the grandeur of Notre Dame and the Louvre, it is a city of art, architecture, and fine food and drink. The great historic sites such as the Place de la Concorde with its grizzly past that saw thousands guillotined during the French Revolution. Walking down the grand avenues and passing the Place Vendome with its imposing pillar and the ornate Opera House were a few of the sites that awed the newcomers to the grand city. The beautiful boulevards and the great department stores mesmerized the young first timer.

And for a very raw country boy like James Hayes, it was like magic. Unlike New York, which they could only glimpse from the Hoboken piers, Paris was there for them. They were part of it. Like a jigsaw puzzle, they could be lost in the neighborhoods of the Latin Quarter with its streets no more than alleys and the great universities that made it a mecca for students and young artists. It was so full of life after the horrors of the trenches and death.

The Latin Quarter, part of the Fifth and Sixth Arrondissment, was a totally different world for county boy James Hayes. It was an area that lured the first-time visitor to its small cafés serenaded by local women in tight skirts, magical looks, and infectious smiles. The seductive qualities of the great city were impossible to ignore. The sights, the smells, and the excitement did indeed captivate the young man from Mississippi.

Ken Levinson had been eyeing the newcomer and knew he made the right decision to take the naïve young man to the big town. It was Ken's first time as well. He had never met his Uncle Marcel, now forty-nine and like his dad, a refugee fleeing the anti-Semitism of the Russian pogroms in 1905. However, Ken and Beau were from big cities. They were amazed at Paris, but unlike James, they were aware of the lures of the city. Ken had to probe his friend. He had brought him here. He felt responsible for him until he could return to his native St. Louis. A reassurance from James was needed. This was the best time to find out.

"So, James," Ken Levinson had to probe, "you like what you see?"

James was like a cat looking into a fishbowl. Wide eyes, looking around at the small quarters, he was like the kid at the county fair who wanted to take the prettiest girl on the Ferris wheel. He wanted to grab and absorb as much of the city as he could. He didn't know where to begin. The looks, the finely dressed men and women walking along the avenues and boulevards, and the dogs that got more attention than any human back home.

What a place. Shaking his head, he responded by using his now-polished English, saying, "This is a magic place. It's so different. So different."

Beau, a city man from New Orleans and the urbane Ken Levinson of St. Louis, found his reaction amusing. They were happy that he was now in the city that would look upon his talents and not his race. This was earth shattering. To be sure, there would be challenges if he stayed, even if that stay would be a short one. Yet here was a place where he could utilize his talent and be appreciated. He was euphoric. Like a first-time kid at a carnival marveling at the Ferris wheel, Paris was his carnival. He would absorb it all.

The city of Paris! How wonderful, how magic, how alluring, especially for the young. The sights, the smells of the crepes, fresh coffee, the pastry shops, the outdoor bistros with and without their dogs, and the people smiling at the Americans who helped win a war just a few months prior. Wearing their uniforms, the three Yanks were greeted in the street by many people with, "*Merci, les Americains!*" James didn't where to look. It was all so exciting for him.

The city was relieved that the costly and catastrophic war was over. Indeed, the French would soon welcome President Woodrow Wilson, naming a street downtown in his honor as he and the other Big Four: Britain's Lloyd George, Italy's Vittorio Orlando, and France's *Le Petit Tigre*, Georges Clemenceau, as they headed to the nearby Versailles Palace to work out a controversial treaty formally ending the Great World War. Decorated with the tricolor French Republic flag as well as the Star and Stripes of the United States, Paris's mood captivated the trio. They felt like heroes wearing their American uniforms.

Walking with Beau and Ken near the Arc de Triomphe, James was taking in the city from the top of the boulevard. Ken had made reservations at a budget hotel recommended by his uncle just off the Rue St. German. It was a walk up three stories to a two-room flat. Its small windows overlooked the West Bank, giving the first-time visitors a good view of the city from the small balcony. It was not far from the prestigious Sorbonne, and the area prided itself as a repository of artists, writers, performers, and *bon vivants*.

Ken had been told by his uncle in previous correspondence to look at the Latin Quarter, and the available walk-up cheap hotels proved to be the best for a first-time visitor on a budget that had to be stretched. It was the perfect niche for a person visiting the city for the first time. More importantly, it was the center of everything a young person would want.

Ken planned on staying with his uncle and aunt at Marcel's home but wanted Beau and James to secure a room for at least a week. Using this small hotel room, Ken felt that James could, after seeing the city, meeting his uncle, and performing at his club, make a more lasting decision. As for Ken, he would leave for his native St. Louis in two weeks. He, like Beau, had someone back home that he wanted to marry. Deep down inside he knew that James was the real deal. His voice, coupled with his good looks and physical presence, would be an instant hit. He told his uncle that the young man had a unique talent and could go solo.

Ken had written to explain the death of the backup singer, Franklin

Duggers, and the possibility of Beau St. Clair not being fully integrated into the group. As far as the music backup group, Ken relayed to James that his uncle had a five-piece jazz band that was the envy of other jazz clubs. Determined to introduce James to Paris, he felt he did all the right moves. Now it was up to James to follow through.

"What do you think?" Levinson knew the Spartan room with few amenities save for an indoor toilet, coal stove, and wash basin would be the norm for the next week.

For James, a poor sharecropper, it was home for the duration. With indoor plumbing, hot water, sink, and stove, it was ideal.

It was his first time away in a hotel or any facility that offered the backwater kid a chance to strut his stuff. Nervous, he reached into his pocket, taking out his now-prized handkerchief. Touching it, he was reminded that his heart was still in Mississippi. He also knew that the last letter that Jane had written for his mother indicated that his family—his dad, mom, and brother—knew he had been a hit overseas. They also knew that James wanted to see Paris before heading back.

In the letter, carefully crafted by Jane Hurley, she wrote, "Your mom knows that you have a special talent, just as I do. For that matter, everyone who has heard that great voice of yours knows, James. She is so proud of you. Your mom wants you to go to Paris, as you indicated. Your length of stay is not important if it means a chance to further your career. She will always have you in her heart and will be waiting to see you at the right time."

He reread this over and over and knew that Jane wouldn't mince her words. He was grateful that Jane would write what was in the heart of his mom. James took a deep breath, absorbing the moment. Looking out the window at the busy street, he turned to Ken and Beau and said, "Yeah, I can deal with this for a spell. Who knows, I actually may get used to it."

With that, Ken and Beau shook hands, and Beau remarked, "We may have made history. When we get back, he might be big. Real big."

Ken couldn't resist adding, "James, don't forget who brought you here! Don't get too big that you forget us."

James walked over and hugged Ken Levinson, saying nothing. There was no need for words.

Ken had explained to his uncle that James would probably end up alone for a brief duration when he and ultimately Beau left for home. Ken's Uncle Marcel was a favorite of the Americans in Paris—Gertrude Stein and partner Alice B. Toklas. Stein was an American from Pittsburgh who had come to Paris in 1905. She became a favorite of art group of ex-patriots who settled in Paris.

One of her friends was the English writer Ezra Pound and the great impressionist artist Henri Matisse. Her flat at 27 Rue de Fleurus became an important meeting place. It was lined with works of modernist artists. Thus, one would find Cezanne's "Portrait of Madame Cezanne," Delacroix's "Perseus and Andromeda," Matisse's "Woman with Hat," and Picasso's "Young Girl with Basket of Flowers." Stein coined the phrase "Lost Generation."

With the passage of the Volstead Act or Prohibition in the United States in 1919, Paris attracted the many artists and writers from the end of the Great World War to the 1930s. A visit to Stein's flat would be testament to the friends she attracted over the years. Hemingway would ask her to be the godmother of his son; Thorton Wilder and Henri Matisse were frequent dinner guests, as were a host of upcoming talent. Eventually that would include James Hayes.

Marcel Levinson also had many friends and was regarded as a fair albeit tough person to work for. His club was one of the most successful and therefore, the talk of the gossip tabloids frequented by many important Parisians. Always in the news, it could be the perfect place for a raw, poor talent to be discovered. Ken felt good that he done the right thing. He also knew if and when he returned to the city, James Hayes would have made his mark. This he was certain of, having seen him perform in person.

In time he would also welcome the writers Ernest Hemingway, Sherwood Anderson, and F. Scott Fitzgerald and his erratic wife, Zelda, over the next three years. Ken's uncle said if all went well and James wanted to stay, he would be delighted to introduce the young, new talent to the displaced Americans. Ken's uncle invited James and Beau to Le Chat Noir that night. Right now, James wanted to get acquainted with his new surroundings and learn the streets in Latin Quarter. He felt liberated. Very soon, he would learn the challenges of Paris as the city demanded of him. However, that would have to wait. Right now, the anxious and frightened young man was about to make his mark on a city that soon he would call his second home. It wouldn't take long.

CHAPTER 20

That night, in grand Parisian style, Ken, James, and Beau were invited to the residence of Marcel and Francoise Levinson. It would be the beginning of a new life for the young son of a sharecropper—a night that would change James Hayes's life.

Greeted at the door by their domestic servant, Lucie Bordeau, the trio of Ken Levinson, James Hayes, and Beau St. Clair were ushered into a large sitting room adjacent to the dining area. *This is as big as some of those white mansions back in Mississippi.* Looking around the wallpaper and fine art displaying some very classical Renaissance art, James felt a bit uneasy. *I've never been in anyone's house for dinner, especially someone with money.*

Beau, smiling at both Ken and James, put the young sharecropper at ease by adding, "We have a few these large apartments in New Orleans. My cousin used to deliver goods, and sometimes, I'd help. But I ain't seen nothing like this, no sir." James thought of Duggers, wondering what he would think. *Probably would say, "There's money to be made in being a big club owner."*

Walking into the sitting room within a few minutes were the hosts, Marcel and Francoise Levinson. James noticed a well-dressed, short, balding man with glasses on while the lady, looking much younger than her husband, was in an elegant black dress. She was at least an inch taller and wore a white pearl necklace with matching set of earrings. Aware of the setting, James stood up, as did Beau.

She said, "*Bon Soir,*" repeating in English, "Good evening," and extended her hand to both Beau and James. Looking at her husband's nephew, she smiled, nodded at Ken, and said in accented English, "You are very welcomed here. Ken has said so many good things about both of you."

Marcel also extended his hand and said, "It's a pleasure to meet you. I know we have a lot to talk about. Tell me, is Paris what you expected?" Before James had a chance to answer, Francoise wanted to get some information from Beau.

She looked at Beau after being introduced and was curious about his background. "*Monsieur*, you have a French name. Marcel tells me you're from New Orleans, yes?"

Beau remarked, "Yes, I'm a Creole—a mix of French, African, and probably American Indian."

"*Tres bien,*" she remarked, smiling and looking at James.

It was James's time to speak up. He had been honing his proper usage of grammar and speaking assuredly responded, "It's so much more, sir. It's a beautiful city. So much to see. If I do stay here, I hope I can fit right in. Just need to learn a little French."

With that remark, Marcel added, "Not a problem. You'll pick it up. It took me a good year to speak it."

"Yes, and he still doesn't have it right," his wife added, laughing. This seemed to break whatever tension or unease was in the air.

"You fellows must be hungry. I know I'm ready for a hearty meal. Let's proceed to the dining area—okay?"

Marcel motioned with his left hand as his servant, Lucie, escorted the guests into an immaculately set linen table complete with glasses and silverware reflective of a feast to come. A beautiful candelabra with lit candles on each end was complemented by a huge vase of fresh flowers from the nearby flower market.

Dinner at the Levinson's that night sealed the fate of James Hayes. His welcome from the family and the introductions to important people on the Paris scene would follow. Over dinner of chicken with white wine sauce and mushrooms, potatoes, French vinaigrette salad, and green beans, Marcel made James a proposal.

"My nephew tells me that I need to hear that fine singing voice of yours."

James glanced at Ken and added, "I like to sing. I'll leave it up to you to see if you like it." James laughed nervously.

"Are you planning on staying in Paris, James?"

"That depends upon whether I can get a job and get used to the city and …"

Francoise, her maternal instincts setting in, interjected, "Let the young man enjoy his dinner first. And then give him the chance to make decisions on his future." With that, Francoise said to her guests, "Eat up, young men. You don't get home-cooked meals too often, do you?"

"No, ma'am, it's a treat," James added.

"Let them eat first, talk later." Francoise was aware that the serious talk would wait until after dinner.

"You're right, let's finish dinner and we'll take a little walk afterward, okay?" Marcel was insistent on getting to know James and finding out his intentions.

Supper over after a great dessert of creme boule, café au lait and assorted fruits, Marcel, James, Beau, and Ken set off to take a stroll in the cool January air.

Marcel got right to the point. "I run a very successful club, young man. I want to get some fresh talent, and I'm going to invite you to come to the club tomorrow with your friend Beau and audition with my band. I have a five-piece orchestra. They are all professionals. I already spoke to them, and they're ready to see you. Are you ready?"

James looked at Ken, who was nodding and almost coaxing James to say yes. James needed no further prodding. Remembering his good manners learned from his parents, he began, "I want very much to audition. It's my dream to make it. If it means Paris, then so be it. At least here, I feel free. And I want to thank you, sir."

The expression on James's face revealed a vulnerable albeit anxious young man—a young man willing to take the plunge and let destiny determine what course his life would take. James, a young man intent on getting his chance to excel, would not think twice. He wanted to feel wanted and not be a pawn. Grateful to Marcel, he held strong to the belief that he had something to offer. *I must have something that they want. I got to try. I got to.*

As they approached a corner café, Marcel suggested they stop in and talk. The four of them, Marcel, James, Ken, and Beau, each shared yet another cup of coffee and relaxed. Marcel, knowing that James's intentions were real, wanted him to know that his stay in Paris might have to be extended.

"If things work out well, I'll see to it that you a comfortable yet reasonable place to stay. Also, I have a friend at the American embassy here on *Rue Royale* who can be of help. Hopefully, once you get a start here, you'll consider Paris your second home. I want you to be happy and not homesick. The last thing I wish for you, James, is to be unhappy. I know what it's like uprooting and leaving home. Your circumstances are similar to mine. By the way, you can go back to America every year and spend time with your family. So if you do decide to stay, I'll do whatever it takes to make the transition easy." With that, Marcel smiled as he put down his coffee cup and waited for a response from James. Marcel wouldn't be disappointed.

"When did you want me to come for the audition?" James felt relieved. "I want to make something of myself. You giving me this opportunity is something I cannot pass up. Thank you, again."

Marcel, a savvy businessman, had set a 10:00 a.m. audition the next day at Le Chat Noir. Rising and shaking hands, Beau and James left for their hotel room, just a few blocks west as Marcel and Ken headed back to the apartment.

"Beau, I think I can do this. I got to try at least." James wanted reassurance from his friend, who was looking down.

Raising his head, he reached out and poked his arm, gently adding, "If it wasn't for you, James, we'd have no group, no music. You the main thing. Yes, you can do this—no doubt, no doubt." The smile on James's face was all that Beau needed. Beau was preparing to leave for New Orleans on the next troop transport out of Le Havre in just a few days. First he wanted to escort his good friend to the audition.

"I'll tell something else. If Duggers was here, he would tell you the same. You know this."

James, the lead singer of what was once the trio, knew this to be true. He realized in Beau he had a good, solid, and reliable person who wouldn't hoodwink him into believing in a task he was unprepared. He would definitely miss Beau once he left. Right now, as they were nearing the small hotel, he turned to Beau. "Just know one thing—you guys, Duggers, Ken, and the musicians are like family. I hope one day we can get together and perform."

Beau had to add, "If you let us, big shot."

Arriving in just a few minutes at the hotel, Beau spoke up. "James, make sure you do right."

"What do you mean?" James didn't know where this conversation was going.

"What I mean is be careful that you don't get stuck here, man. You may not want to. I hope it works out for you, but just saying, make sure, make sure."

James appreciated his friend's concern and shook his head, adding, "Oh, I will, I sure will." Exhausted by the drama of the night and the possibilities that awaited him, the wine started to take hold, and soon James was sound asleep.

Morning came too early. James had a fitful sleep, realizing that tomorrow would be one of those special days. He had to be real; he had to be ready, and he prayed that all would go smoothly. His recurring dream was hazy. The woman in the white dress seemed distant but still warm and inviting him to join her on a stage. "Maybe, just maybe, she's my guardian angel. I used to be afraid that she was the angel of death while we were fighting in the trenches. But she always had a glow and warmth about her." James just hoped she was a good omen for his big debut that would change the course of his life.

Getting dressed after a quick shower, he got Beau up and toasted some French bread with butter and heated up water for the coffee. The small facility had well-used utensils. The forks and knives and plates had, no doubt, a history that could communicate quite a story. James placed a napkin and two forks and knives for Beau and him and poured the coffee before Beau finished a quick shower.

"It's 9:10. I want to be out of here by 9:30." They would have to take the Metro or bus across the Seine to the club. Normally, it would be a twenty-five-minute walk or a ten-minute subway ride. James felt invigorated. The open window provided a nice breeze to complement the singing of the sparrows in the nearby trees. He looked out and smiled. It was a clear, crisp late January day, and the walk would do him good. Besides, he wanted to time himself. If this was to be his route to the club, he wanted this to his test.

Beau and James arrived a few minutes early at Le Chat Noir. Both Ken and Marcel were there and escorted them into the main room.

Typical of the 1920s Paris clubs, its outside neon sign of a large black cat was juxtaposed with the names of the players on stage. Coming into the entrance, he could see that every attention to detail was achieved. Immediately, the red carpets, plush red drapes, and rounded tables with matching red lampshades caught the eye of James. It was a warm feeling. The stage was large enough to accommodate a dance group. The orchestra was in the recess area. Already, one of the musicians, a saxophonist, was tuning up. James, ever the observant one, liked the club and knew a lot of time and money was put into it. Marcel had recruited three of the five musicians from America, assuring James that he would feel at home, with no language barrier. Indeed, with the possibility of Prohibition being passed by the US Congress and enacted into law as the Eighteenth Amendment, many professional club musicians would take one of the many steamers and cross the pond. This would be better than risking the uncertainty of having nightclubs back home closed. As a result, Paris, as early as 1919, was welcoming some American musicians. Since Marcel had the largest and most successful nightclub in Paris, musicians tried to audition for a spot at Le Chat Noir. Indeed, several American notables had already performed to the delight of the war-weary Parisians. Among them were the popular Bricktop and composers Eric Satie and Darius Milhaud. Marcel's club was the place to be seen, and entertainment writers from Le Monde and

Le Figaro frequently wrote a friendly column on the great jazz coming out of Le Chat Noir. His Montparnese club was a real hit. James didn't fully understand what Ken had done for him until this moment. He entered a new world—a world that would forever change his life. He reached into his pocket, just to touch his good luck handkerchief, and said a silent prayer. "Sweet Jesus, if this if meant for me, let it happen, let it happen." He wouldn't have long to wait.

CHAPTER 21

James stepped up on the stage and was introduced to the five-piece orchestra: Tony, a drummer from Cleveland, Jacques, a native Parisian pianist, Mike, a saxophonist from DC, Louis, a native Parisian flutist, and Joe, a guitarist from Boston. They made up a jazz ensemble that had already gained fame and was recognized by Parisian society. Marcel had several singers but had no one who stood out. He was in competition with the other clubs that gave Paris its unique appeal.

He took a chance on James, based on his nephew Ken. As he remarked to his wife, "At least I'll give him a chance. He could always go back to Mississippi."

Marcel already had a passport issued for James and a visa working permit. A good judge of character, he looked forward to the audition.

No one knew what to expect as the nervous, not quite twenty-year-old singer stepped on stage, least of all James. He wanted not to fail Ken, Marcel, and most of all, himself. *I'm going to pretend I'm singing back home at church or to the troops.* That thinking worked before when entertaining the troops. He was sure it would work here too.

The band's leader, Jacques, said in halting English to the newcomer, "Just sing like you always do." Jacques could see the gleam in James's eyes. He had observed him awed by the surroundings. He liked what he saw—James had groomed himself well—clean, new shirt compliments of Marcel, and a matching pair of slacks and black patent-leather shoes.

He looked the part. He looked relaxed despite the butterflies in his stomach. He smiled at Jacques, thanking him for the welcome.

Marcel knew first impressions meant a lot. He told James that the band could play anything, provided it was standard jazz piece. James knew that this audition would be closely followed not only by Marcel but also the orchestra. Slipping into the audition were two staff members—a waiter and a coat-check girl. They stood in the back out of sight. They had heard that a newcomer was about to sing. They had seen others come and go and knew it was a do-or-die moment for the young upstart. They wanted him to succeed. By staying near the exit doors, they would go unnoticed in the dim light-café club.

It was determined that he would sing a standard. His tenor voice had a big range, and he knew he could do it. The orchestra started up. In the audience, sitting in front at one of the many red tablecloth top tables were Marcel, Beau, Ken, and the night manager, Claude Genet. Since Beau was leaving in two days, it was decided that James would do a solo number. Beau looked at him as he was about to begin. James reached into his pocket, gently touching his good luck handkerchief.

The band's music began a nice mix of jazz and blues. They asked him what song he wanted to sing. He chose a popular standard of the day. The band started tuning up, and Beau gave him a thumbs-up, forcing a smile from James. He was ready.

Feeling confident, James began his singing act. He sang, his voice rising, and got Marcel to sit up straight. Looks were exchanged by Genet and Levinson. Good vibes with a real soulful sound were emanating from the young singer.

The number, followed quickly by another popular jazz mix, got the band members moving to the rhythm. James began to move with the music. His stage presence started to shine. He moved his arms and gave Marcel a free show that was unique in style. His pitch and range were right on target. He was very comfortable. The musicians, giving an occasional glance to each other, knew that something special was happening. History was being made by a twenty-year-old American transplant.

James, transported in mind back to his small, poor country church, was giving a solo performance the likes of which was never heard before. *This young man has destiny in his hands*, Genet thought.

After the third song, "Margie," Marcel stood up, quickly followed by the other three at the table, applauding. Joining in the applause were the band members and the two staff members in the rear. James had arrived!

Marcel came up to James. "James, I think in time you'll master the French language. So, let me be the first to say—as owner of Le Chat Noir—*bienvenue, mon ami*." Placing both his hands on his shoulders, he repeated, "Welcome, friend." James's smile said everything. He and Marcel hugged, which caused Beau and Ken to rise and do the same. Genet congratulated the young man, telling him he had been to many auditions and this far exceeded them all.

They knew he had that special voice. The band had stopped, placing their instruments in their cases, and descended down to the floor. Each of them shook hands and introduced themselves formally and welcomed him in traditional Latin style with a peck on each cheek. James had indeed arrived.

Before deciding on a big debut within a month, Marcel had his wife secured a lease in a nearby upper-level flat. Annette Martin was the owner of several small flats. She was a trusted patron of the club and a friend of Francoise. The apartment she selected for James would have all the amenities that he didn't enjoy in his native Mississippi. He would have his own bathroom, shower, small stove, and a comfortable bed that he could call his own. And like Paris during this decade, *Les Annees Folles* or Lost Generation, it had American artists and writers who abandoned the United States temporarily with the passage of Prohibition.

Marcel paid Annette in advance for the first three months. It was an outright gift. Marcel was a great businessman and knew James was going to have a quick rise to fame. He didn't take from James what would be his salary for the rent. It was his way to thank James and his American nephew, Ken.

Aware that James was raw, naïve, and not accustomed to the big city, he wanted to have a short lease, be near, and make sure he was not vulnerable. He kept him on a short leash. Marcel, with two grown children on their own, welcomed the chance to be a surrogate father to what he hoped would be the latest sensation in Paris jazz circles. His investment in James Hayes proved to be most lucrative. He didn't want the temptations of the city to compromise this great discovery.

James Hayes couldn't believe his luck. At age twenty, his gifted voice would be recognized by all circles. From the wealthy to the working class, James was destined to become famous. Like it or not, fate dictated his destiny. His meteoric rise to fame became the talk of the bistros, restaurants, and clubs.

Over the next two months, he honed in on his routine and worked diligently at the club for ten hours a day. Yet, not all was perfect. With the absence of Beau and Ken, he was alone and lonely. He would walk along the Seine and see young couples, hand in hand, exchanging kisses and smiling at him. He would smile back and wonder when he would be in the embrace of a nice young woman. Even the drunks seemed happy to him absorbed in their own world.

One night, after a brief spring rain, he walked along the wet embankment along the Left Bank. His refection appeared in the puddles as he walked. He suddenly felt very alone. Under the famous bridges with their signature initials of Napoleon, he stopped and took a deep breath. He had friends, a career taking off, and a support system from Marcel. Yet, something was missing.

He would carry his trusty handkerchief and think of his family, and it would help boost his spirits. Paris was a gracious lady that could also be tough and uncaring. She was also a very seductive city, beckoning native and visitor alike to appreciate her and tempt her at every whim. James had friends at his flat, at work, and would soon be a favorite at Gertrude Stein's parties. People recognized him from the pictures and posters on the street announcing his big debut date.

Told by Marcel to be on his guard against the "barracudas," he was always cautious whenever a young lady would pass her number to him at the club. He was singing a song or two every Friday, and already crowds were coming in. He was getting used to the club and comfortable before crowds. Marcel wanted to have his routine down lest the critics have a different take. Marcel had taken James under his wing. He looked out for him. His good looks, fine statuesque physique, and wonderful smile would make him a real catch. Yet Marcel had to warn his young protégé, "Some of them will flaunt their name and number in front of the men who escorted them." Marcel wanted James to know that with celebrity came notoriety. These were the individuals he wanted to avoid.

He was homesick, writing to his mother via Jane Hurley. In one letter, he explained what it was like to be alone in his room, "I should be happy to have a career and get noticed. My big date is just a few days away. But I miss my family, and I wish you could be here. My handkerchief, silly as it sounds, is my connection to the family I love and miss."

James went on to add that he had acquired friends in the building and in the club. He would have dinner every Sunday at the Levinsons' home. They were perfect hosts. He liked Marcel, and he knew he owed his career to him. His meal ticket was in his hands and his confidence in him. Yet, he was coming of age in a city that prided itself on its youth, art, music, cuisine, and love. The lack of racial hostility in a more tolerant Paris was such a contrast from back home. It was a catalyst that clinched his desire to stay here and make it. He acquired the skills needed in a jazz club. He was a quick learner, and Marcel moved up the date of his debut, making corrections on the posters in the Left Bank bistros.

His big day arrived with a full house, thanks to Marcel's networking with the newspapers. Paris was abuzz about the new talent. The transplanted Americans living in Paris like Gertrude Stein and Alice B. Toklas and an array of curious jazz aficionados crowded the club, awaiting the debut of the young American. Marcel had James introduced after the dance troupe entertained the crowd. It was now his turn.

James came onto the stage. Dressed in a rented tuxedo, his youthful, handsome presence immediately resonated with the crowd. He began a medley of jazz songs familiar to the patrons of the club. The silence was deafening. His Sunday gospel singing had come across the pond and was now captive to an audience intent on his every word. He didn't disappoint. His voice soared with raw, soulful emotion only a few could achieve. That night would change him forever. James Hayes had captured Paris, and it was his for the taking. And the people flocked to the club.

Within a few months, James had his photos splashed all over the tabloids and was a sensation. Walking about in the city, he was recognized. He was starting to learn a little French. Humorous as his accent was, it was nevertheless appreciated. The club's staff liked him very much. He wasn't affected and bloated by his instant fame. He treated everyone the same. His humble upbringing and sense of fair play stayed with him. He started making the club money, and Marcel increased his take-home pay. He sent money every month via international Western Union to Hurley's, knowing the honesty of Ms. Jane Hurley. By the beginning of 1920, he was interviewed by both *Le Monde* and *Le Figaro*.

His apartment had photos of him from the newspapers placed on the wall. His neighbor, an aging prostitute who called herself Mimi, became a good friend. She would warn him of those barracudas, as did Marcel. "They are out there just to use you." After seeing him with a questionable sort, Mini decided to speak up.

In her halting English, Mimi would ask, "That girl I saw you with is not good for you. She has been around a lot and takes and takes."

James by mid-1921 was in Paris for over two years and away from Mississippi for nearly four years. Although only twenty-two, he had several love affairs. Each of them was short-term. Mimi, not the nosy type, looked out for him, and he became a loyal friend. "I just can't find the right person for me. Better if I just enjoy the moment and forget about any marriage or kids."

Mimi told him to take it slowly; she was a seasoned person at forty-three and wanted James to continue to excel with his career. He got her a permanent seat at the club and introduced her to Gertrude Stein and her partner, Alice. They liked her honesty and devotion to James. Deep down inside, he was a lonely, young albeit talented and famous performer. He would have the recurring dream of the angel with the white dress. He dismissed it as just a sentiment or momentary lull.

He tried hard not to get hurt whenever he got emotionally attached to the females who were always there. Some of the ladies were great and became friends, but something was missing. He was still a country boy deep down inside who yearned for stability and not one-night affairs. Mimi kept reminding him that he would know real love when it hit him. "*Mon cher*, you will fall over one hundred percent! Just make sure she's the right one."

Throughout 1922 and 1923, James's career excelled. His rendition of "Sheik of Araby," "China Boy," and "Roof Blues" were huge hits. He had been in France five years and wanted to visit his family. His career gave him the opportunity to get a larger apartment with his own cook. Yet, he was still a young man who got lonely. Mimi remained a good friend and visited him often. He still went to the Levinsons' for Sunday dinner.

He had many friends but no one steady. He had been burned a few times by trusting the wrong woman. In one instance, some possessions were stolen. Nothing much—a few francs plus a cheap watch. This and other events made him reassess Mimi's advice. After that incident, he was more circumspect, more cautious of people in public.

He had his handkerchief, which was a linkage to his roots. He decided that in 1924 he would travel back home. His salary was again increased, and he got offers to perform at the Palladium in London and in Berlin. Side trips to the French Rivera during the traditional August vacation time gave him some relief from the city's heat. Staying in Nice, he was recognized wherever he went. The time spent there was therapeutic, and a few plunges in the warm Mediterranean proved to be invigorating. Meeting some of his Paris friends, he had dinner at the summer home of Ernest Hemingway and was guest of honor at the mayor's house. He still thought of home. He had now been away a long six years. Now, at age twenty-four, he had so much to offer.

Then, one night in October 1923, a beautiful young brunette came to the club in the company of her parents. She sat in the front row to see Jimmy Hayes, as the French called him. The scent of her perfume, although not overpowering, was evident. A recent graduate of art at the Sorbonne, she wanted to hear the voice that sent this young man to meteoric heights and was the toast of Paris. She had listened to his voice on the Victrola. She kept a scrapbook of his career. At home, she had all the articles in the Paris art section of the daily newspapers. The young fan appreciated his rise to fame and likened it to the evolution of an artist, starting slowly and eventually getting recognition.

She had pictures of him and kept copies of the posters that flooded the Left Bank when he first came to fame three years earlier.

Her parents surprised her for her twenty-third birthday by taking her to Le Chat Noir and made sure that they had a front-row seat. For the event, she bought a new dress and belt. It was a white sheen dress with a very bright red sash.

CHAPTER 22

Her name was Marie Benoit. At twenty-three, she was already a successful art graduate and employed at the Louvre. Her position as assistant manager of the Renaissance collection was demanding. The prize masterpiece, Da Vinci's "Mona Lisa," was in her charge. Her love of Renaissance artists transcended into the music world. Marie Benoit also was a lover of jazz. She and her friends would frequent some of the small bistros with live jazz and stop along the Seine listening to impromptu groups of musicians. She wanted to hear the now-famous Jimmy Hayes. Her parents granted her that wish as part of her birthday present. Her visit to the club would be a life changer for both her and James Hayes.

Listening to James Hayes was the highlight of her night out with her parents. She didn't let her eyes off him. By the time his performance ended, their eyes met.

Told by the manager that there were a few birthday observers in the audience, James had everyone join in singing "Happy Birthday." He then asked the birthday people to rise to applause. Marie, in the front row, caught his eye. When James looked at her, he nearly let out an audible gasp.

Marie Benoit had a new white dress with a red sash that she had purchased just for this occasion at the famous department store on Rue Hausmann, Les Galleries. Like most meticulous shoppers, she had tired on a blue dress followed by a red dress. The white sheen dress caught her eye. She favored blue, but her eyes keep going back to the white dress with the distinctive red sash.

She smiled at James, and he nodded. Was she the woman in his dreams? It couldn't be. But he wasn't going to let her go. Not just yet.

After his routine, he was invited to sit with the Benoits at their table. Marie's father, Pierre was a successful importer. With piercing black eyes, moustache, and jet black slick hair parted in the middle, he reminded James of a Chaplinesque figure. Her mother Helene, part Egyptian and French, still showed her beauty with a coiffed dark black hair complemented by a sleek black dress she wore very well. As he approached the Benoits' table, Monsieur got up.

Introducing himself to the group wasn't necessary, but James had impeccable manners. He graciously kissed the hands of the ladies, pausing a moment when it came to Marie. "Happy Birthday, Mademoiselle."

She smiled at him, adding, *"Merci bien, Jimmy."*

Mrs. Benoit told James, "My daughter is wild about you. She has all your pictures."

Marie smiled nervously, adding, "Monsieur James, you are my favorite."

The waiter poured a glass of Merlot for James and raising his glass, added, "Here's a toast to Mademoiselle Marie on the occasion of her birthday." Clinking glasses, Marie smiled at James, and he followed up with a wink.

Small talk ensued about art, music, a bit of history, the war, and finally Marie's job. Discussion about Marie's position at the Louvre prompted her to ask, "Would you like to stop by and see our latest displays?" James knew this was a clue for him to jump at the chance of meeting her again. He didn't need to think to respond. After all, this was the woman in the white dress!

"I'd like that very much. I've been to the Louvre only once before. I could use a good art history lesson. Thanks." Marie was looking at his good looks and blushed a bit when he caught her smiling at him.

James and Marie started to become an item in Paris society. Her parents liked James's very warm and courteous manner. Marie's mother,

Helene, was very reassuring, telling James that she had some difficulty when first meeting her husband. "Some of Monsieur Benoit's relatives didn't like the fact that I wasn't French and although I was raised in France, questioned my loyalty. In due time, they came around. So, young man, don't worry what others say or the occasional looks when you're with my daughter. You are a beautiful couple, and I'm delighted to see you in her life." James very much liked Madame Benoit. As an Egyptian with dark features and Christian Coptic roots, she was not totally accepted at first by Marie's family. In time, that changed.

Educated at the Sorbonne, she was a very wealthy clothing designer. She knew fashion and was a consultant to the major fashion spreads in Paris. Respected for her expertise and sense of flair, she doted on her daughter, making sure she always looked her best.

In fact, it was she who suggested that Marie buy the now-famous white dress she wore that very night at the club. Given a special status at the department store, the white dress was yet to premiere in the windows of the famous store. So, it was a very special dress.

A classy lady with many friends in Paris society whose husband was very wealthy, she soon became a fixture at society events, such as being in charge of fundraising for the French army during the World War. She hosted several successful events at both the elegant Opera House and at the Louvre. Appearing with the mayor of Paris, Madame Benoit made sure that the lowly troops suffering and dying in the abyss of the trenches were not forgotten. After the war, she energized much of her time to make sure that the wounded were attended to. Often visiting hospitals and rehab clinics, she kept the money flowing despite the postwar inflation. When she looked at James, she saw a bit of herself—a person who had to prove himself and be accepted based on talents. The bonding grew stronger, and her husband knew that the couple was destined for each other.

By early 1924, Ernest Hemingway and fellow American transplant F. Scott Fitzgerald and his wife Zelda were asked to host a party at the apartment of Gertrude Stein. James had requested that Stein's flat, large and in the center of the Left Bank, would be the perfect venue for a special announcement. That night, January 12, James Hayes and Marie Benoit were engaged. The party went on for hours with plenty of food and drink. James wanted to marry in the spring, and it was arranged that a civil ceremony, followed by a church wedding. Reaching into his handkerchief, he silently whispered, "Wish you were here to see this, Mom."

Raised a Catholic, Marie wanted to respect his Baptist roots and didn't insist on a church wedding. James had no problem with any ritual. He was a transplanted American who had come to appreciate French culture. He wouldn't give up his roots or forget his background but wanted to please his wife-to-be. He asked his mentor and dear friend Marcel Levinson to serve as his best man. Also, Hemingway and Fitzgerald and two of his band members would serve as hosts or ushers.

The wedding was held on April 27, 1924, at the Iglise de Madeleine, the stately church at the top of the Rue Royale. The press was out in full force, and the church was filled to capacity. James wished his parents and brother could be there. They would be so proud. He reached into his tuxedo pants, making sure his ever-present handkerchief was there. A link to his Mississippi roots, he smiled and pictured his mom and dad sitting proudly in the front pew. He thought of Duggers, Beau, and Jimmie Ray. He wished they could have been there for him. For a moment, he felt like he wished he were in his little country church instead of the stately and ornate church with its beautiful stained-glass windows, statues, and Grecian columns. Filled to capacity, the wedding of James Hayes and Marie Benoit was the event of the spring. But this was his day. And Marie's. The organ began the wedding march, and he looked at the procession of bridesmaids followed by Marie.

Marie, escorted by her father, came down the aisle dressed in white. She also had a red sash around her waist. When James caught sight of this, a broad smile came over his face. *She was and will always be my angel.*

Many of James's extended "family" were there too. Gertrude Stein, Alice B. Toklas, the authors Sinclair Lewis and F. Scott and Zelda Fitzgerald, and the famed painter Pablo Picasso were guests. Many fans were outside and were anxious to see the couple emerge after the ceremony. The press, eager to get pictures, was given a section in the back of the church. They wanted a spread in the tabloids by the same evening edition. The wedding was the talk of Paris, and the press competed for the best pictures.

A gala reception took place at a private room of the Maxim's just down the street on the Rue Royale. Catered by one of Paris' finest restaurants, the guests feasted on a variety of gastronomic delights. From the pate de fois gras to coq au vin, wine and assorted pastries, the guests were entertained by the band from Le Chat Noir.

James escorted his wife to the stage and sang the new hit from American composer Hoagy Carmichael, "Star Dust." The guests loved it. He followed up by jazzing up the crowd with another new hit from America, "Hard Headed Hannah" and "Riverboat Shuffle." Marie, with the help of the backup singers from the club, sang "The Man I Love." The guests loved this public display. Even the staid Marcel got up and danced with the new bride. So did Hemingway. When Gertrude Stein, her not-too-small derriere swinging to the beat, got up and did a solo act, the crowd loved it.

"Amazing what a few glasses of wine will do to old Gertie," Hemingway laughed. Marcel and Francoise, acting as surrogate parents, made sure that all went smoothly.

James and Marie posed for the photographers, formed a receiving line, and danced their first dance. It was, in the worlds of Hemingway, "like Paris a feast unmatched."

James and Marie left for a honeymoon to the Amalfi coast of Italy, south of Naples. They took a first-class train car to Rome and then transferred to Naples, where they boarded a cruise ship to take them to Positano on the bay of Naples.

The rugged Italian coastline with its picturesque villages and sunbaked white roofs contrasted to the gray and baroque buildings of Paris. James took a deep breath and said to his new wife, "Who would ever imagine a poor, backwater kid from Mississippi would marry the most beautiful woman in Paris." Marie grabbed James and gave him a kiss on board before disembarking for the honeymoon suite at the resort's largest hotel. Inside the suite was an array of flowers sent by Gertrude Stein and another from Marcel and Francoise Levinson.

The town embraced the honeymoon couple, giving them the gastronomic treats that make Southern Italian cooking so legend. Recognized by both natives and tourists alike, they were treated like royalty whenever dining out. Meats such as veal, pork, and fish served with pasta and wine became a staple for their stay. The desserts topped with an occasional gelato were daily treats.

Enjoying the cuisine of Southern Italy and sightseeing by going to the Isle of Capri and the famous Blue Grotto and the ruins of Pompeii, the newlyweds spent two weeks touring before leaving for Rome via Naples. In Naples, they had a chance to see the ornate San Carlo Opera House across from the beautiful Galleria. Once in Rome, they stayed two nights near the Spanish Steps in the same hotel that the poet Keats stayed overlooking the Via Condotti. Their view of the Tiber with the Vatican in the background was the perfect setting.

Visiting the treasures of Rome, like most tourists they had the famous gelato at the Piazza Navona and spent a day visiting the Coliseum, Vatican Museum, and St. Peter's Basilica. Marie had been to Rome several times; she made sure they threw coins into the Fontana di Trevi. James had never been to Rome and was overwhelmed by the ruins of the Forum. By the fifteenth day of their honeymoon, they were on the express train back to Paris.

Returning home, they moved into new and larger quarters on the Left Bank. James, at age twenty-five, married with a good income and fame, had achieved so much—more than he could ever have imagined. His faith in God plus the values that were instilled in him from the hard, often unfair, and demanding life back home made him grateful. His mind would wander back to Mississippi. He hoped that the years had been kind to his parents and they were able to get some relief from the funds he sent. Guilt coupled with pride made up his psyche. He was a happy man and had achieved beyond his wildest expectations.

He continued to send money to his parents and was relieved that, at long last, they could leave their wretched existence on Crawley's land by renting quarters off the Crawley property. He could now send money directly to them via Western Union. They had mail delivery at their new address. Grateful to Jane Hurley, he stayed in touch with her, remembering her May 4 birthday, sending a card. He also included a check for Jane, who had always been there for him from the time he was a child. Remembering her fairness to his people, he had a special place for Jane Hurley. Mutual sentiments were exchanged; Miss Jane always smiled whenever she thought of James.

Thanks to his generosity, James provided for his family. His dad was smart and saved enough to move his family. His mom now had indoor plumbing, hot water, and indoor bath and toilet facilities. His brother's asthma was improving with age, and he was now dating a local girl. He missed seeing his folks. Yet, he knew many of the people back in Hinds County were worse off than his parents, and he was indeed grateful that he could at least provide for his them. He spoke to Marie of visiting Mississippi in the coming year—1925. She encouraged him to visit. They wouldn't have to wait long.

CHAPTER 23

Seven months into their marriage, a telegram arrived at the Hayes residence. It was from Jane Hurley asking James to consider coming home. At the suggestion of his mom, Jane sent the telegram with an urgent request.

His dad was diagnosed with terminal stomach cancer and given only three months to live. It was November, a slow period at the club. The summer tourists had gone, and there would be ample time for him to finally book passage on a liner and get to Mississippi for a few weeks. He wanted to go but not under these circumstances. Marie poured a cup of coffee and set down a baguette for him.

After he handed the telegram to Marie, with tears in his eyes, she read the message. "I'm so sorry, James. You got to go. It's your dad. You always talk about how a good man he is. I don't want you to have any regrets if he dies. You know you would say the same if it were my dad in a far place."

James looked at Marie and gave her a kiss on the cheeks. He didn't like the distant look in her eyes. She didn't look directly at him. It was as if she was not revealing something. *Is there something she's not telling me? Marie is always open with me.*

"Marie, I know that look. Something is on your mind. Tell me. I don't have to go all the way to Mississippi. We talked about an open marriage ..."

Marie blurted out, "I'm pregnant! I'm due in late June. I was going to prepare a nice dinner and tell you on Friday. But this news from your family …" She stopped in midsentence.

James got up from his chair, smiled at his wife, and said, "Well, this is a day of mixed news. I'm going to be a father! Yeah, me a father."

Marie kissed her husband, adding, "All the more reason why you should go now before I get on with this pregnancy. You'll be able to spend some time with the family and be home by Christmas." James could see that his wife made sense. He would have to book passage to New York from Le Havre and then take a train to Mississippi. They would entail one week each way across the Atlantic plus a day or two layover in New York and at least two weeks with the family. It was November 3. He would have a chance to book passage for a November 6 crossing. He was glad that he kept his passport updated plus his work visa. He would go later that day to a travel agent on Rue St. Jean and book the passage. He was in luck, as a ship was due to leave in two days.

That afternoon, James booked passage on the *George Washington*, the passenger ship that had served as a troop transport during the World War. It was also the same ship that President Woodrow Wilson sailed for Versailles in 1919 to negotiate the controversial Treaty of Versailles, ending the war.

James got a second-class cabin with a balcony. Since the ship would set sail in just two day; he gathered all his documents and, with Marie's help, was able to pack for an expected four week trip. He stopped to purchase some gifts for his mom. Marie selected fine lingerie consisting of a house dress plus a plain albeit black sheen dress. Knowing his mom's dress size, Marie was able to have the contents carefully wrapped. She also put in a personal note to his mother. As always, he folded his special handkerchief, placing it in his right pocket.

The night before his departure, he and Marie had a long discussion. He explained what life how different life was in the delta. Sensing his nervousness, she repeated several times, "You're going to be a father, just like you have a father to see back home. I want your daughter or son to know their father. You told me of the horrible situations there; please, be careful, James."

Marie arose and went to the stove and prepared the dinner she had anticipated before the news from overseas arrived. She had some of James's favorite foods: pork chops, assorted vegetables, potatoes, and a dessert from Maxim's. Simple comfort food that seemed so appropriate for this night.

Leaving his wife in her condition made him uneasy. Marcel and Francoise plus Gertrude Stein and his friends all indicated that they would look after her. Of course, Marie had doting parents who would also be there for her. Marie's mom was concerned about her son-in-law's safety. She also had heard of the life in the delta and wanted James to be careful, now knowing that he would soon be a father. Francoise Levinson knew of the lynchings and brutality against blacks and others. She wanted her son-in-law to be aware that he might be a target, given his notoriety. He assured his in-laws that he would always have Marie's best interest and the fact that he wanted to see his baby born.

James boarded an early train to Le Harve and then boarded the stately ship. His quarters were luxurious compared to the troop transport that brought him over during the war. He had a balcony and a large bed in the second-class quarters. Marcel tried to upgrade him, but due to the late booking, all the first-class compartments were taken.

The ship left port on a drizzly, cold November morning and headed for New York, some seven days off. He settled in, took a shower, and proceeded up to the restaurant. James was recognized by both the Americans and the French. Asked if he were performing in New York, he was candid in telling them of his family situation. He had received a telegram that morning on board that his father's condition had deteriorated; he just hoped he could make it down to the delta before it was too late. But the company on board was a respite from the harried life of Paris. He sent Marie a telegram from the ship indicating that he was on his way and that, despite the rough sea for the first two days, the sea was now calmer and the quarters he was assigned to were more than adequate. He slept soundly.

Two days before they arrived in New York, he was approached by the ship's event programmer, Marge Harwood. She was a big fan and asked James if he would sing one song at the closing show. He mentioned the circumstances of his trip. She backed off, but then James, having second thoughts, decided that a diversion might be the best thing. It would also give the poorer third-class passengers an opportunity to hear his velvet voice. Many of them were fearful immigrants who were subject to the new laws passed by Congress restricting further immigration from Southern and Eastern Europe. Some were fearful of deportation. He accepted and practiced his now-famous number "Star Dust" with the band's orchestra. It was a surprise and hidden treasure for all to see.

His performance was a stellar event. Not only did he sing "Star Dust," but he got the band to play several other jazz numbers. The audience loved it, giving him a standing ovation. He was invited to sit at the captain's table the next day as his guest and was given access to the first-class restaurant. His time aboard the ship was reflective of the appreciation of the crowd; many wanted to know if he was going to stay in New York. They hoped that he would have an engagement at the Waldorf or at Roseland Ballroom. But James Hayes had other issues on his mind.

He was coming to an America that had rejected the Versailles Treaty, turning its back on the world. President Wilson resorted to a more isolationist stance. The United States would never join the League of Nations, the genius of Wilson's Fourteen Points. The United States's reluctance to join gave rise already to a Fascist regime under Mussolini in Italy and threatened the stability of the Weimar Republic in Germany with the rise of Nazism.

The passage of the Volstead Act had backfired. Instead of curing alcoholism, it brought about organized crime to a public intent on drinking in the private clubs or speakeasies cropping up in the United States. As Hemingway, cup of wine in hand, aptly summed up to James one night at the club, "You can't legislate morality. This will be a complete disaster." And Hemingway, never one to mix his words, was right on target. The failed experiment also brought about "homemade brew" and moonshiners in remote parts of the country.

Coupled with this was the fundamentalist "monkey trial" that would soon grab headlines whereby a Tennessee biology teacher, John Scopes was put on trial for violating state law in teaching Darwinist theory of evolution. The United States, despite its victory in the war and giving the women the right to vote, had backtracked on other issues. The urban versus rural conflict would continue for decades.

This was the 1920s in America that also saw the enactment of restrictive and intolerant immigrant laws that were aimed at Catholics and Jews. With the influx of new immigrants from Italy and Eastern Europe, the Congress passed and President Coolidge signed the quota system that severely restricted immigration from those areas. As a result there was an increase in the KKK with intimidating racist marches, lynching, and in-your-face outright challenges. James was aware of what was going on and knew he was about to enter the fray.

He arrived in New York and within two hours was headed south. The overnight train would have him traveling through the Carolinas, Georgia, Alabama, and Mississippi. He had to change to the "colored car" once arriving in Virginia and remained there for the next twenty-two hours until he arrived in Jackson. He had to adjust to his new surroundings and remember he was a black man in the South. He was called "boy" for the first time in six years.

In Jackson, he was met by his cousin Lonnie and went immediately to the house he helped rent for his parents. The family was aware of his homecoming, and a large contingent of twelve people awaited his arrival. The aroma emanating from the kitchen was the result of the church ladies who wanted their famous native to enjoy good country eating. They had prepared fried chicken, okra, macaroni and cheese, and homemade biscuits. James inhaled deeply, walking into the home he had helped his parents rent. There were many of his friends present. Included in the mix were Charles Atwood, Jane Hurley, and even Jimmie Ray Owens.

James went up to his mom and hugged her for what seemed a long time before entering his dad's room. His father was propped up with two pillows. James could see the extent of the illness; he had lost so much weight and was just holding on. He held his dad's boney hand and spoke with him and his mom privately for about fifteen minutes. He showed pictures of his wedding and told his dad he was to be a grandfather in June. His dad was smiling, despite his obvious discomfort. The doctor had prescribed small doses of morphine to ease the pain, and it was evident that he had just days left.

James's mother took him aside, saying, "He was always talking about you to anyone and everyone son. So proud, so proud. Remember where you're at now, son. This ain't Paris. It's still the same old Mississippi. Don't you forget it."

James grabbed his mother, her eyes tearing up, and escorted her outside the bedroom to the waiting long table set up by the ladies group of Zion Baptist and sat down and began to eat a very hearty meal. He looked up at the wall with pictures of his success in both the local and international magazines. He was home.

CHAPTER 24

Jeremiah Hayes died on November 17, just two days after his son's arrival. He was just fifty years old. The funeral was held on November 22 at the church. Filling the pews were his family, friends, and some press from Jackson. Surrounding his casket were large floral wreaths from Paris by Gertrude Stein, Ernest Hemingway, and his in-laws, the Benoits. Francoise and Marcel wired money to James's mother in memory of his father. His mother wore the black dress that was picked out by Marie. It fit her perfectly.

The program for the funeral of Jeremiah was entitled "Journey Home." Jeremiah had a dark suit with a red tie and a white carnation in his left lapel. The undertaker performed a good job, making the emaciated corpse look presentable to the public.

Included in the program was a special spot—a solo performance with the choir in background. The soloist would sing "How Great Thou Art," and it would be followed by a eulogy by the Pastor Atkins.

James was surprised to see none other than Warren Crawley enter the sanctuary and speak to him and his mom. Crawley looked all of his sixty-four years. James, surprised by his presence, looked twice to make sure it was old man Crawley. *Good Lord, I thought I'd never see him pay respects to any of us.*

"Your dad was a good man. I will miss him." James couldn't quite understand how a stoic, mean-spirited man like Crawley could show up. But remembering his upbringing, he shook Crawley's hand as the landowner prepared to leave. Crawley went over to Lula Mae and said a few inaudible words as James was receiving others in the line. James noticed that he went directly out without acknowledging the many people who worked for him in attendance. This was his first surprise at the service.

Many others came and went before the service began; many decided to stay. His friend Charlie Atwood showed off his now four-year-old daughter, Annie. James proudly told him of his pending fatherhood and showed off his wife's picture to Charles. Next in line was Jane Hurley. He was intent on seeing her before heading back to Paris. Grateful to have her presence, he wanted to thank her for all she had done by putting herself up for scrutiny by the "good old boys" who loitered at the store.

Jane Hurley got a big hug from both James and his mother.

"We are so grateful for all you did for my Jeremiah. You always read those letters from James. I hope we can continue."

Jane took Lula Mae's hand, reassuring her, "Don't ever worry. As long as I'm able, I'll be there for you and your famous son." Smiling, she gave James a big hug.

He remarked, "Ms. Jane, after the service, I hope to come by in a day or two to the store. I have something for you from Paris." Ms. Jane was all smiles despite the somber setting and proceeded to her seat in the rear of the church. James had some perfume he bought for his mom and Jane Hurley. *Wish there were more like her.*

Jimmie Ray was the only other white person to pay his respects. He spoke to James, telling him that he had gotten his driver's license and was working with a local distributor out of Vicksburg. He was married with a son. He and James spoke of their time overseas and decided to meet in a few days.

Also present was his Uncle Moses, who came down from Chicago for his brother-in-law's service. When James spotted him, he went up to him, saying, "If I never got drafted, I probably would have come up to Chicago."

His uncle, shaking his head, quickly added, "You did better, son.

The family is so proud of you. I'm glad you made to your daddy's service."

He gave his uncle a hug. He explained that his wife, Ruth, was unable to get down due to recurring bouts of arthritis. "I understand. I hope one day to do a gig there. I hear you have quite a town with Capone and all."

Moses brushed aside his hand, adding, "You don't want to mess with that crew. No way. Wait till this prohibition nonsense ends." He proceeded to his seat.

James's brother, Nathaniel, with his girlfriend Geneva in tow, sat next to Lula Mae in the front pew. James sat on the other side of his mom. James looked about the small, country church in which he was raised. *So simple yet so beautiful.* He was used to the stately, ornate Gothic cathedrals in Pairs. He was grateful to God that he made it home before his dad passed.

The service began with a hymn followed by some scripture readings. Then, the pastor asked James to come forward to sing his dad's favorite hymn, "How Great Thou Art."

His voice soaring, the congregation rocked with the rhythm. The backup choir added to the glorious tribute. James's mother sang along with the congregation. Soon, some were up on their feet, waving their arms and moving with the motion. By the time he finished the hymn, the entire assemblage was clapping on their feet and moving in a rhythmic trancelike state. James had scored once again, this time for his dad.

A eulogy was given by the pastor. In it, Pastor Atkins spoke of his humble beginnings. "The son of a slave, he remained true to his roots and family. He stayed in the same house that he was born in. He worked on the Crawley land as a loyal sharecropper despite the hardships of sustaining an accident. Yet, his family was everything."

The pastor went on to explain that his sons had both overcome the obstacles of Jim Crow South by applying themselves and succeeding. His brother, Nathaniel, had overcome childhood illness. He was employed working full time in a factory nearby. Pastor Atkins then spoke of Jeremiah's wife, Lula Mae, and the trials she went through.

"Despite his injury, she always encouraged him never to give up." The congregation interrupted with "amens" several times. Atkins concluded that their famous son never forgot his roots and wouldn't let obstacles stand in his way. "James, like his parents, is strong in spirit and body. He won't give in to injustice or unfairness. This is what is needed by us. And James, like his dad, never, never gave up the fight. He knew who was real. That tribute is evident by this large crowd paying respects to a simple but humble man who never gave up." With that, the crowd applauded as the coffin was removed and the choir sang, "Amazing Grace."

After the interment, a large spread of food was provided by the ladies auxiliary of the church. The ushers made sure everyone was fed. James was able to reconnect with many of the people he knew as a child. The young ladies marveled at his good looks and sighed when told he was now married. One of his former admirers remarked, "If his wife be here, she be in trouble with all these young ladies wanting to talk to James."

That evening, at home, a few people trickled in who were working and couldn't make it to the service. Jimmie Ray stopped by to say hello. He wanted to find out how long his buddy would be staying. When James explained that he had to get back to Paris to his wife and restart his career at the club, Jimmy informed him that in the area the Klan was reorganized and sights of cross burnings in the next county had occurred. There were rumors that an illegal distillery was discovered by a few local black kids and they were beaten and threatened.

"Just be aware that this place hasn't changed, James."

The pattern of segregation, cemented by the *Plessy* decision of the Supreme Court, wasn't going away. The federal government was too busy trying to prosecute bootleggers from New England to the Appalachians.

The FBI, formed in 1908, didn't target injustice in the segregated South. It allowed the states latitude when it came to crime. Many crimes committed in the states seldom involved the Department of Justice or the US Attorney General. Looked upon a as a state issue, lynchings continued well into the twentieth century. By the 1920s, there was a resurgence in the KKK. The FBI and its new chief, J. Edgar Hoover, were more intent on going after Chicago gangsters and breaking up the lucrative and illegal flow of liquor coming across the Canadian border.

Appointed by President Coolidge, Hoover put his priorities in areas where headlines would be made. He wanted attention. He wanted control. He had little time for state crime, regardless if they violated constitutional rights. He was the game, and he was in charge.

He wanted headlines like capturing "Pretty Boy" Floyd and executing John Dillinger. Hoover didn't aggressively go after those who were committing heinous racist lynchings. That was a local crime, and the states had to deal with it despite the cries from the NAACP and civil rights groups and progressive Northern politicians. These crimes didn't make national headlines, except in the black press. James indeed knew he had to be careful in this scary climate of racial divide.

James would need no warning from anyone. He could see the tension from the train rides to walking around the area. From the time he entered the Deep South, he was forced in a segregated car and called "boy" more than once. And when he had to use the "colored" rest room, his guard was up. He appreciated Jimmie Ray's concern but knew that he had to get back to Paris. The life he had now was vastly different from just seven years prior. He could see for himself more clearly now than ever the extent of the Jim Crow South and the degradation by deferring to the white inhabitants. He wanted nothing more than to get his mom out of here but knew she would never leave.

Within a few days, he sent Marie a telegram announcing that his return ship would be leaving New York in just three days. He should be home in eleven days. It was November 24, Thanksgiving Day. He had booked passage on the *George Washington* for November 27. He hoped to be in Marie's arms by December 5. It would never happen.

CHAPTER 25

James Hayes was on his way back to Paris via the train north to New York and the liner *George Washington*. It was November 25, the day after a sumptuous Thanksgiving dinner at home. Masking her grief well, Lula Mae kept busy with the help of Nathaniel's girlfriend and prepared a dinner that would have made her husband proud. Thanksgiving was difficult for all the family, but they were blessed to have James in their presence, however briefly. She had inquired about Marie. He laughed when he told her of his recurring dream and the angel in white and the good luck handkerchief.

"Son, the Lord works his way, works his way."

Saying good-bye to his mom became another emotional moment. He told his mom he would get her a passport and have her come to Paris. She hesitated, brushing aside her hand, saying, "Lord, I haven't been out of the delta but once, son."

It was time to leave. Jimmie Ray had his truck and would take him to the next town for the night train up North. James's mother didn't like the idea of him traveling at night. "You be careful, and don't make any noise. Remember where you are, son." With that, he kissed his mom and said good-bye to his brother and headed out the door for the long trip to Paris. She stared at him and stayed outside the door until the truck carrying her son was out of sight.

Jimmie Ray had asked if he needed to stop before they got to the station for some candies or any snacks. Being white, Jimmie Ray could enter into the shops marked "white only." James had a nice basket of food. Some of it was from last night's big Thanksgiving dinner. "Thanks, but I got enough food to last me all the way to New York." Jimmie Ray arrived at the station with James and bid him good-bye. James was aware that Jimmie Ray, now married, had to get home.

Giving his friend a hug, Jimmie Ray added, "Y'all come back, ya hear." James turned and smiling, ascended the three steps and went into the small station.

Like small train stations giving sporadic service to all points in the US, the station had but one small ticket window that was closed. A single aisle separated the pew-like benches on each side of the aisle—marked "whites only" on the right and "colored" on the left. The bathrooms, also segregated, were at opposite ends of the station. No posters, no billboards, no advertisements—it was indeed a stark and Spartan place. The dampness in the air permeated the station. James noticed that the few people there had on their coats. He also noticed no refreshment stand. If he wanted a cool or hot drink, he'd have to wait until he boarded the train.

Since it was a holiday weekend, the station had only seven passengers—three to the left in the "whites only" section while a mother and two children were in the "coloreds only" section. The children were sleeping soundly. The place was eerily quiet for a station, and the stained floors were in need of cleaning. The odor was musty and foul.

There was no one working at the ticket counter. People could purchase tickets once boarding, and in the rural South, there were few passengers traveling at this time of year.

The train was scheduled to leave overnight at 10:00 p.m. When James inquired about the schedule, the woman with the children shook her head, saying, "There's a three-hour delay." No notice. The woman said she had a friend who worked on the lines and knew it was going to be late. *It's Mississippi, and I got to remember that.* He thanked her and sat. He reached into his pocket and held his handkerchief almost as if it were a religious icon.

James got antsy sitting there. He used the "colored" bathroom and decided to get some night air. He passed by the white section where the four people were sitting. One of them, an elderly man, looked him over. James gave him a friendly nod with no response. *I'll be glad once we get North and I sit where I want and feel free.*

Stepping into the cool, late November air, James wanted to get a bottle of pop, as soda was called here. He walked a few paces and saw a neon light several yards down the deserted road. It was a night convenience store, and he decided to head in that direction. He could see that it was a gas station from the one pump there. He hoped that the proprietor was on duty and he could get some soda.

Out of nowhere, a car with three young white men braked just up the hill from the station and within sight of the store with the neon light. He stopped. The car pulled in front and screeched on the brakes. He could hear the laughter from the men inside.

He didn't have his bag, as the lady with the children said she would look after it. James asked if he could buy her a bottle of pop for her and her children. She said she would be grateful.

He knew something was up, as all three got out of the car. They were young, perhaps still teenagers. Their leers and swagger were evident as they approached James.

"Where you going, boy?" asked one of them, which prompted laughter from the other two.

"I'm just on my way home. Needed to buy some pop at the gas station." James looked them square in the eye. He didn't like the tone of their voices. He knew he had to get out of this situation fast. "Look, I'm heading up north, and all I want is to get some pop. I see the light is on and I'm sure it's open …"

"What's the matter, boy, you don't like our company?" James saw a bottle of hooch in one of the men's hands. He knew that homebrew could be strong in these parts. Prohibition was the law, but that hardly stopped the men in rural America from supplying people in the cities.

"Wouldn't you want something stronger than that sissy pop?" The one carrying the bottle came up into his face and asked, "You got some money?"

James had a wallet with $120 on him to get him to New York and a cab and possible hotel overnight. He also noticed that one of the men went into car and produced a shotgun.

"Look, men, I'm not looking for trouble. I just needed to get some air and—"

"I asked you boy if you had money. Do you? Maybe we should have worn our hoods!" The man with the shotgun had his gun raised and hand on trigger. They were acting irrational, probably drunk. He had to be very careful.

"You got some ID on you?"

The one with shotgun noticed a wedding band on James finger and said, "I see you married, boy. Don't want your lady to be a widow, do you?" James, alone and on a deserted road with a bunch of rowdies, didn't want to escalate the situation. The odds, he knew, were against him. Instinctively, he reached into his pocket, touching his handkerchief.

"Let me see your hands, boy. I don't know if you got a knife or pistol …"

"I don't. All I want any trouble …"

Laughing, the one with the rifle, feeling his power asked, "You got a picture of your lady?"

James could see the situation was getting out of control. With young, cocky drunkards intent on scaring him and having a picture of a white wife, there surely would be trouble. He had no recourse but to run the short distance down the hill to the small train station.

James turned and started running hard toward the station. The guy with the shotgun had it pointed, laughing, and started running after him. Suddenly, he tripped. He had his hand on the trigger. The gun went off, hitting James in the back. He fell hard. He was dead instantly.

"What the fuck did you do? We only wanted a few dollars. He's dead all right. I don't need to tell you that, fool!" People from the station heard the gunshot and started coming outside.

"I didn't mean it. I had my hand on the trigger, and I slipped."

"You idiot! Get the fuck in the car now. I'm not doing time for this, no way, no way," the driver said, rubbing his hands.

"Get your ass in the car, both of you." The driver, a sandy-haired man of just twenty, was nervous, repeating his orders. He wanted to act quickly. He knew he had to.

The man who shot James was a local drifter, as were the other two. They were making moonshine and distributing it. They lived two counties away and were in and out of trouble since their teens.

Two of the three had criminal records ranging from petty thief to illegal bootlegging. One had served in the federal penitentiary for six months. And they had just finished a job and celebrated too much at the illegal distillery a few miles down the road. They had a lot of moonshine in the trunk of the car. It was illegal and subject to federal charges. The sheriff could arrest them for bootlegging and then question them about the circumstances surrounding the death of James Hayes. The driver knew he had to act and act very quickly. He wanted no evidence. Since he had been in trouble before, he decided it wasn't worth the effort to take the money from James's pocket.

"Let's get out. Don't touch him. They'll have fingerprints, you jerk. So get away and get in the car now!"

The car sped away as one of the waiting passengers came upon James, looked him over, and shook his head. "Poor man didn't stand a chance." The car already was out of sight, not giving the witness a chance to describe the make of the car or get the license plate number.

The man shook his head as he looked at bloody sight. It was the same man who had stared at him in the station. He ran back inside the station and called the police from a pay phone inside. The woman watching his suitcase screamed when she heard the news. It awakened her children, who saw the abject fear in their mother's eyes.

"I pray the Klan isn't coming here too," she said aloud, shaking her head. She prayed for the nice man whose possessions she had and prayed for her and her children. "I hope it ain't the Klan," she repeated several times.

The sheriff arrived and questioned the four adults in the station.

They all agreed that they had seen James step out and then heard a loud shotgun blast less than fifteen minutes later. The sheriff went out with his deputy and called for an ambulance. Knowing that the shot was a fatal one, he told the dispatcher to send the county coroner over at once.

CHAPTER 26

James's body was removed to a local funeral home until his mother could be notified. The sheriff came to her door at 4:00 a.m. "Oh no, no, it can't be my James," she sobbed. The sheriff asked if she needed a ride to identify the body. But by this time, the word was out that James Hayes, who had just buried his father, was murdered

She and her brother got Jimmie Ray to take them to the funeral home. They were ushered into a small back room that was used for embalming. James lay on a cold, metallic slab. His body was covered with a white sheet. The sheriff and the funeral director looked at Mrs. Hayes. He looked at the sheriff, who gave him a nod to proceed. Mr. Jones, the funeral director, gently uncovered the sheet, showing James Hayes. Lula Mae collapsed in Nathaniel's arms. Jimmie Ray let out an audible curse and walked out, weeping. No words were exchanged. There was no need. Her cries plus the sobbing by his brother and Jimmie Ray confirmed their worst nightmare.

The news would spread quickly across the Atlantic. Getting a call in the middle of the night, Francoise awakened her husband, who knew the news couldn't be good. "Who the hell calls at this hour?" When his wife told him that James Hayes was killed, he arose from his bed and banged his hand on the nightstand, shouting, "Those bastards. Those bastards!" Marcel knew what he had to do next. Getting dressed, he mismatched his socks in the confusion and raced downstairs. He hated the fact that he would have to tell Marie the dreadful news.

Francoise, knowing that a female presence might help, quickly dressed, insisting, "I'm going with you too."

"Oh no, no! Not my Jimmy! Not my Jimmy!" Marie fell into the arms of Marcel. Francoise, already in the kitchen, was preparing coffee and making calls to friends despite the fact that the clock showed 4:32 a.m.

Marie Hayes, inconsolable in her grief, was in no condition to be alone with a newborn due in June. Francoise, after bringing in some coffee and baguettes, held her hand. Marie kept repeating, "What did they do to my Jimmy?"

Glancing at her husband, Francoise said, "Call the doctor now."

Marie was totally despondent, and the doctor was called in to administer a mild sedative. Her parents came and people from the inner circle from the club, and notables like Gertrude Stein, Ernest Hemingway, and the Fitzgeralds all came. Hemingway was especially indignant. "What is wrong with those idiots? His career taken by a few ignorant white hicks!"

Hemingway, grabbing Gertrude Stein, held her a long moment. The somber atmosphere in the Hayes apartment matched the grief across the Atlantic. Soon there was a constant flow of support for Jimmy Hayes from the people who loved him.

Gertrude Stein and Alice Toklas took over for the despondent Marie. They received guests, ushering them into the parlor. Stein ordered food and drinks for the steady stream of mourners. Once regaining his composure and tempering his outrage, Hemingway handled the press and the growing crowds outside the apartment. The news of Jimmy Hayes's death was broadcast on the radio. It spread quickly throughout Paris.

The press, the radio, and the French public wanted answers. On the front page of the normally staid and straight-laced *Le Monde*, the headline read, "Jimmy Hayes—a Victim in His Own Land." Everyone in Paris seemed to react in their own way. People walking by the apartment left flowers and notes for Marie as a tribute to their adopted son. A radio reporter asked people why they came, and the response from one young woman summed it up nicely, "Jimmy Hayes inspired me. He opened up the music of his people, and I got to appreciate it. I shall miss him so much—so much."

The French ambassador asked for an explanation and wired President Coolidge. He asked the FBI director, J. Edgar Hoover, to look into the murder. It took a week before the communiqué reached his office. When he was told that Hoover wasn't concerned about the murder of a black man, the ambassador, Jacques Le Grand, a frequent patron of the *Le Chat Noir*, blurted out, "What did you expect from him?" Apparently even the French knew the FBI chief was more concerned with rounding up bootleggers than looking at injustices in the Jim Crow South. The ambassador's outrage reflected the love, respect, and concern for James Hayes. Now, in this dark hour, they too wanted answers.

Soon the streets of Paris would see a memorial at the base of the Arc de Triomphe with a large picture of Jimmy Hayes and hundreds of flowers. Ordinary Parisians of every age reacted to the event of the delta.

Services were held, Masses said for his soul, and Jimmy Hayes became a tragic albeit loved figure. His picture was splashed onto the papers, asking, "What's going on in Mississippi?"

The investigation into his death led nowhere. Outrage, anger, and injustice all surrounded the premature death of one of the most famous jazz singers of his age. The local district attorney ruled the death a homicide, but with no one coming forth, it became a cold case. Private investigators could only speculate that a group of young men, wanting to rob and intimidate a black man, led to murder. It remained unsolved. When Lula Mae had responded, "Somebody knows," it remained an elusive cold case in the South in 1924. Nothing new. Given the notoriety of the crime and the fame of the person, it had no effect. Just another black man killed.

The men responsible kept surprisingly quiet, especially when they found out that the victim was a world famous jazz singer. Two of them fled Mississippi and went up to Memphis and got jobs. One died at thirty-one of alcoholism. It was rumored that he wanted the truth about James's death told.

It wasn't until 1977 that the case was solved. One of the men involved, on his deathbed at age seventy-four in Knoxville, made a Baptist death conversion and told in stark details the facts.

"We just wanted to scare him and take a few dollars. I tripped, and the gun went off. I hate myself for that. That's why I'm telling you all now. I need to come clean. I so need to come clean." Those were his last words.

Speculation that the Klan had something to do with the death of James Hayes added fuel to the Jim Crow injustices of the South. The NAACP asked the US Justice Department to investigate. The FBI, more concerned with gangsters both nationally and locally, did nothing. Hoover wasn't going to get involved despite the fact that a world-famous entertainer was killed. The black newspapers and radio kept the murder of James Hayes on the front page for months. Soon other issues prevailed, and the death of James Hayes would be history.

Yet his music continued and started to be appreciated on this side of the Atlantic. With the advent of radio coming into homes in the 1920s, he achieved in death what eluded him in life—respect in his own part of the country. Love of his music and his voice soon made James Hayes a popular and yet tragic episode of the story of America.

When they removed James's body, he had his hand in his pocket. He had just wanted to touch his handkerchief. His mother made sure that the handkerchief was sent to Marie. She kept it for her newborn son, James Marcel Hayes, who was born on June 2, 1925.

Marie agreed to have James's body buried next to his father. It would be too much for his family and his mom to have the body sent to Paris and buried in the famous Pere Las Chaise.

His funeral was not only a tribute to him but also a public event that involved national and international media. It was broadcast on local radio and picked up by the Chicago affiliate of NBC. Thousands stood outside the small Zion Baptist Church to pay their respects. Black and white, rich and poor, they wanted to come. Ken Levinson came down from St. Louis. He and Jimmie Ray and several of James's cousins served as pallbearers.

Through it all, Lula Mae held up well. Having lost a husband and son in the short span of a few weeks, she displayed the dignity and character that had sustained her all these years.

Like most poor black sharecroppers in the delta, she had grown stronger over the years. Never losing her pride and the family unit that was so important, when asked by one of the mourners that they didn't know who did this, she retorted, "Somebody knows. I ain't gonna rest till I know."

The land that had claimed so many had now claimed James Hayes. The delta always looming overall. The land was lord, and it now added the famous young upstart who had impacted the world so much. The delta, the soil, the land of the wet and angry river still held its grip over everyone. It wouldn't let even the most talented and most determined to break away. Once again, as in the past, the land's power couldn't be matched. James Hayes ended up interred in the very soil he abhorred, next to the fresh grave of his dad.

James Hayes, one who succeeded in leaving the delta, ended up in her grip.

Lula Mae Hayes would eventually get pictures of her new grandson and felt proud that her son had achieved so much in such a short life of twenty-five years. As she said to one of church ladies, "He should have done more. He was gonna do so much more." Proud, dignified, and respected, she was emblematic of the many Southern women who had endured so much.

Paris named a club in James's honor. They invited a young St. Louis woman who was influenced by James's music who wanted to join the ever-increasing migration of singers, writers, and artists to Paris during the 1920s. She wanted so much to meet him

Arriving in Paris in April 1925, just five months after James's death, she was asked to perform at the newly named jazz club—Jimmy's Place. She stepped to the microphone. She had on a white dress with a red sash. She composed a love song entitled "Jimmy Hayes." Her name was Josephine Baker.

CPSIA information can be obtained at www.ICGtesting.com
Printed in the USA
BVOW08s1840190716

456124BV00001B/17/P